Y0-CBL-974

"You could have booked into a motel."

Sara flung the words at him. "Instead of trying to push in here!"

Leon growled in a low voice. "Even you must realize it's the holiday season. I couldn't find alternative accommodation."

"How shall I explain your presence in the house? What are the neighbors going to think?"

"Surely—not the worst?" Leon teased, grinning broadly. "We'll have to see what can be done. We musn't let them think I'm jumping into your bed every night."

Sara's cheeks reddened as she gasped. "That's most unlikely to happen. You'll not crawl into my bed—"

"You're right. I never crawl. I usually stride in and fling back the covers while the maiden utters wild cries of ecstatic anticipation."

Miriam MacGregor began writing under the tutelage of a renowned military historian, and produced articles and books—fiction and nonfiction—concerning New Zealand's pioneer days, as well as plays for a local drama club. In 1984 she received an award for her contribution to New Zealand's literary field. She now writes romance novels exclusively and derives great pleasure from offering readers escape from everyday life. She and her husband live on a sheep-and-cattle station near the small town of Waipawa.

Books by Miriam MacGregor

HARLEQUIN ROMANCE
2931—RIDER OF THE HILLS
2996—LORD OF THE LODGE
3022—RIDDELL OF RIVERMOON
3060—MAN OF THE HOUSE
3083—CARVILLE'S CASTLE
3140—MASTER OF MARSHLANDS

Don't miss any of our special offers. Write to us at the following address for information on our newest releases.

Harlequin Reader Service
P.O. Box 1397, Buffalo, NY 14240
Canadian address: P.O. Box 603,
Fort Erie, Ont. L2A 5X3

THE INTRUDER
Miriam MacGregor

Harlequin Books

TORONTO • NEW YORK • LONDON
AMSTERDAM • PARIS • SYDNEY • HAMBURG
STOCKHOLM • ATHENS • TOKYO • MILAN
MADRID • WARSAW • BUDAPEST • AUCKLAND

If you purchased this book without a cover you should be aware
that this book is stolen property. It was reported as "unsold and
destroyed" to the publisher, and neither the author nor the
publisher has received any payment for this "stripped book."

Original hardcover edition published in 1992
by Mills & Boon Limited

ISBN 0-373-03225-0

Harlequin Romance first edition October 1992

THE INTRUDER

Copyright © 1992 by Miriam MacGregor.
All rights reserved. Except for use in any review, the reproduction or utilization
of this work in whole or in part in any form by any electronic, mechanical or
other means, now known or hereafter invented, including xerography,
photocopying and recording, or in any information storage or retrieval system,
is forbidden without the permission of the publisher, Harlequin Enterprises
Limited, 225 Duncan Mill Road, Don Mills, Ontario, Canada M3B 3K9.

All the characters in this book have no existence outside the imagination of
the author and have no relation whatsoever to anyone bearing the same name
or names. They are not even distantly inspired by any individual known or
unknown to the author, and all incidents are pure invention.

® are Trademarks registered in the United States Patent and Trademark Office
and in other countries.

Printed in U.S.A.

CHAPTER ONE

SARA sat at the reception desk, her pen poised over the list she was compiling. The salon was silent, having closed at midday for the weekend, and she told herself it was only the lack of subdued chatter, the muteness of the hairdryers, that made the place feel haunted by clients and staff who would normally be there. Yet the uneasy sensation of being watched continued to creep over her, until at last she looked up to meet the intense stare of a tall man standing on the other side of the glass door.

For several long moments her gaze locked with brown eyes set beneath dark brows, then she noticed the thick dark hair with its glint of auburn and its slight wave. She flicked a glance over broad shoulders clad in a tan shirt, then lowered her eyes to the task of making out an order to be sent to the wholesaler.

But now her fingers gripped the pen more firmly. She was not accustomed to being stared at in this manner, although a thought at the back of her mind registered the fact that he was one of the most handsome men she had seen. But why had his scrutiny of her slim form and blonde hair held such intensity? Did it mean he was assessing her ease as a pick-up?

If so he could forget it. She did not allow herself to be picked up by a stranger, even if he did look like one of God's gifts to women. And then her thinking became more rational as she realised he was probably a visitor to this holiday resort set on the shores of Lake Taupo. No doubt he was here for the trout fishing, but in that case why wasn't he out on the lake?

Or was he a man in search of a haircut? After all, it was a unisex salon, but couldn't he see that the place was closed? Pam and Dawn, her two assistants, had already left, and she herself had remained only to make out the list to be ordered. Had he come to meet Pam or Dawn? Yes, that was it.

The thought sent her to the door, which she unlocked and opened without removing its short chain. 'Are you looking for somebody?' she queried through the narrow gap.

His deep voice came in a lazy drawl. 'Yes, you could say so.'

'If it's Pam or Dawn I'm afraid they've left. We close at midday on Saturdays.'

'But you're still here,' he said pointedly.

'I had a task to complete.'

He looked at the gold lettering on the door. 'Salon Sara. I presume you are Sara?'

'That's right. Now, if you'll excuse me——' She tried to close the door, but was unable to do so because his foot kept it open.

'You'd shut the door in my face?' he rasped.

'Kindly remove your foot!' she snapped.

'I'd like to talk to you——'

'I've no wish to talk to you. I don't know you——'

He grinned mirthlessly. 'You will, lady—you will!'

'Believe me, I'm not even remotely interested—and if you don't remove your foot from the door I shall yell for the police!' she snapped.

'You do that. I reckon it'll give them a laugh,' he retorted in an unruffled manner.

'Why should it do that? It's their job to protect people from being molested by cheeky strangers.'

'You don't look too molested to me,' he drawled. 'Not a hair out of place. Besides, I'd tell them we're living together.'

'Which is a lie you'd find it difficult to prove,' she hissed, infuriated by his temerity.

'You think about it,' he advised in a cold tone.

'Don't be ridiculous! I couldn't *bear* to think about it. Now please remove your foot.'

As he did so Sara closed the door with a slight bang. The encounter had shaken her, and as she returned to the desk her legs felt weak. She lifted her pen, but now the task lacked concentration and she found herself writing for shampoo instead of perming solution.

Nor could she recall which hair tints should be replaced, and this caused her to leave the reception desk and make her way to the shelves in the back room. While doing so she refused to allow herself to glance towards the door, but when she emerged she realised the space outside the front entrance was empty. A sigh of relief escaped her, and returning to the desk she completed the order.

She left a short time later, glancing about her as she did so, and feeling thankful there was no sign of the man in the tan shirt. The depressions of the previous week were still hanging over her head, and she was not in the mood for small talk with strangers. Keeping a brave face in front of the clients had been difficult enough, and now, as she hurried towards the car park, her thoughts went to the cottage she would in future occupy without the company of her great-aunt Jane.

However, her ponderings came to an abrupt halt when she reached the car park where her small elderly green Datsun stood waiting. Nearby, with superiority written all over it, stood a white Daimler, and as Sara caught sight of the man sitting behind the wheel she was forced to catch her breath. It was easy to recognise the tan shirt and to realise he was that same irritating man who had stood outside the salon door.

Nervousness gripped her as she realised that he was watching her. Had he guessed she would make her way to the car park? Had he been waiting for her to do so? Of course not. She was being ridiculous. But as she drove along the highway bordering the northern shore of the lake the rear-vision mirror told her that the white Daimler had also left the car park and was not far behind. Surely he couldn't be following her?

'OK, Mr Tan Shirt, I shall put you to the test,' she told the reflection in the mirror, and, reducing speed, she turned into a lakeside parking area. 'If you have anything further to say to me you may stop and do so—but no way shall I allow you to follow me home to see where I live.'

However, her fears appeared to be groundless, because the Daimler shot past without any sign of stopping. Sara breathed a sigh of relief, and to give it time to make distance she sat and watched the children playing on the narrow pumice beach.

The January sun, giving midsummer heat to New Zealand, sent sparkles across the two-hundred-and-thirty-eight-square-mile expanse of water where fishing launches rode the blue surface, and as she closed her eyes against the dazzle her thoughts returned to the cottage, and then to her great-aunt's solicitor, Mr Abernethy.

She was assailed by a twinge of guilt as she recalled that twice the elderly man had requested her to visit him. The first request had been issued the previous Monday at Great-Aunt Jane's funeral, when, after muttering a few words of sympathy, he had said, 'Come and see me as soon as possible. There's the matter of her will.'

'Oh?' Sara had looked at him through tear-blurred eyes. 'I think I can guess what's in it.'

'You're sure about that?' He had failed to look at her while his tone had become dry.

'I've been given to understand—I mean, Great-Aunt Jane always said——' She had fallen silent, feeling the time inappropriate to be speaking of an inheritance.

John Abernethy had continued to avoid her glance. 'I'm positive Mrs Patterson would wish me to make sure you understand its terms. You'll make an appointment to see me? It's important.'

His words had floated over her head with Sara scarcely hearing them. She had been fighting the inward battle of choking back sobs while assuring herself that Jane—

as her great-aunt had preferred to be called—wasn't really in that long box with all those flowers piled on top. It was only her shell. Her soul was elsewhere—Sara hoped, with her dear Samuel.

However, the following days had been busy, with numerous people coming into the salon for attention to their hair. Sara had felt unable to leave the workload to Pam and Dawn, and the time had slipped by. And then the second request had come from Mr Abernethy.

It had taken the form of a letter which had arrived yesterday, and it had suggested an appointment for nine o'clock on Monday morning. It had also betrayed his anxiety to see her, and this had puzzled Sara. Did all solicitors bustle matters along in this manner? She had already indicated that she had an idea of the will's contents, because Jane had never made any secret of her intention to leave her entire estate to Sara.

And now, still sitting with her eyes closed, she recalled the elderly woman's pleas. 'You will take care of the cottage for me? I've kept it maintained in memory of Samuel, and I'll trust you to carry on with the good work,' she had said.

'Yes, of course I'll take care of it,' Sara had promised. 'But please don't talk about dying.'

'Nonsense, we must face facts,' Jane had declared. 'We both know I've turned eighty, and we both know the time will come when I'm no longer here. Which is why I'm making this stipulation.'

'Stipulation?' Sara had queried the first time it had been mentioned. 'I don't understand——'

Jane's mouth had become firm while she had stared into Sara's hazel eyes. 'I want you to promise that when I've gone to join my dear Samuel the cottage will be maintained—*properly*.'

'Yes, of course.' Sara had licked dry lips.

'You must watch for wood rot on the south side, and for any borer. The cottage is like me, it's old. Now then, promise me.'

'I promise,' Sara had said, nodding while glancing at the faded living-room wallpaper which would soon need to be renewed.

The timber-built cottage was shaped like an oblong box. Its paintwork of deep red with white facings emphasised its earlier period, almost causing it to look like a misfit beside its more modern neighbours. The small entrance hall and passage gave access to three bedrooms, a bathroom, the living-room and kitchen. Gables rising above the front bedroom and living-room windows removed the austerity from its façade.

'And there's the herb garden,' Jane had pursued. 'The chives must be divided at the right time and the mint must not be allowed to run riot. Borage seedlings must be transplanted before they become too large. You'll promise to keep it cultivated?'

Again Sara had nodded, finding herself unable to speak.

'It has such a variety of herbs, and so many of my friends call in for a sprig of parsley or sage. Nor is it known as Rosemary Cottage without reason. Samuel's mother always gave departing guests a few stems of rosemary. Did you know that rosemary is for remembrance?'

Sara had sent her great-aunt a fond look. 'Darling Jane, I shall never need rosemary to remember you. I shall never forget your kindness to me.'

Jane's lined face had broken into a smile. 'Well, it's cut both ways. You came to me when my dear Samuel died. You brightened the days of a sad old woman.'

'But you helped me too,' Sara had reminded her quietly.

Jane had brushed the suggestion aside with her usual down-to-earth abruptness. 'Oh, yes, I know we came together just after you'd finished a silly affair of some sort, but you were sensible enough to get *that* fellow out of your mind.'

Sara had sighed inwardly. '*That* fellow' had been Terry Purvis, and although she never mentioned his name the humiliation he had caused her still held a bitter hurt. Even now the recollections were painful, and while switching on the ignition to continue the journey home she tried to brush them aside.

However, as she approached the small lakeside dwelling they were swept completely from her mind by the unexpected sight of the white Daimler standing parked on the roadside. She ignored it as she entered the short driveway, but before she could open the garage door the man was at her side. She stood still, facing him uncertainly while waiting for him to speak.

His deep voice rasped on a note of irritation. 'You've taken your time in arriving home!'

'So what?' she flared.

His mouth thinned. 'I saw you turn into that lakeside parking area. Was it a deliberate ploy to keep me waiting?'

'*Waiting?* For what?' Sara demanded.

'To talk to you, of course, Miss Masters.'

Startled, she realised he was aware of her surname.

He went on, 'Weren't you expecting me to turn up sooner or later?' The question came drily.

She shook her head, frowning thoughtfully. Had she forgotten something? It was quite possible, because there had been so much on her mind during the last week, then, looking up at the tall stranger, she said, 'Why should I expect you? I have no idea who you are.'

He gave a slightly mocking bow. 'Leon Longley, at your service.'

She continued to look at him blankly.

He frowned. 'The name doesn't ring a bell?'

'Not even a tinkle. Why should it?' She felt disturbed, because there was something here she didn't understand. The shock of finding him at the house was beginning to have an effect, making her legs feel weak and causing an inner trembling that forced her voice to become unsteady.

He shoved his hands into the pockets of fawn trousers encasing long legs. 'Jane wrote asking me to come for a weekend,' he informed her nonchalantly.

Sara stared at him incredulously. 'I don't believe you.'

'You're accusing me of lying?' The question was clipped.

'It's possible,' she retorted coolly. 'Can't you see that if Jane had invited anyone to stay for a weekend I'd have known about it? Surely you can understand that simple fact.'

'Perhaps she forgot to tell you.'

'Nonsense! Despite her years Jane was as sharp as a dart. Nor do I believe she'd invite a stranger into the house.'

'A stranger to you, perhaps, but not exactly a stranger to Jane. Actually, she suggested I could give her an idea of the value of this property. I happen to be a property developer.'

'I'm sure any of the local estate agents could have done that small task,' Sara pointed out coldly.

'Nevertheless it was my opinion she sought,' he returned loftily.

Sara's voice became scathing. 'Unfortunately you're too late to give it to her. If you'd come last weekend you could have stayed over for her funeral—so now you'll understand why I don't believe all this codswallop about an invitation.'

'Ah, but you don't realise it's now several weeks since she wrote to me.' The brown eyes were examining Sara's face with an intensity that embarrassed her.

She turned away from him. 'Is that a fact? Yet you saw fit to delay your arrival until now.' If this man imagined he could wriggle his way into her house by the process of admiring looks he could think again, she decided.

His voice held a note of weariness. 'I spoke to her on the phone. I explained the various projects that were delaying my visit. She understood that as I live in Auckland I was unable to drop matters at a moment's notice.'

Sara echoed disbelief. 'Yet she didn't see fit to mention the arrangement to me. Why would that be, I wonder?'

He shrugged. 'Who knows how the female mind works?'

'I can tell you why,' she snapped angrily. 'It was because the arrangement didn't exist, of course.'

His mouth tightened. 'Again you're suggesting I'm a liar. Thank you very much,' he gritted in an icy voice, his eyes glinting with anger.

Sara took a deep breath as her eyes slid over the athletic form standing before her. 'I really don't know what to think about you, Mr Longley. I must admit to feeling somewhat confused.'

'Why not ask the lady next door what to do?' he suggested with a touch of irony. 'She's watching us from behind her curtain.'

Sara felt a surge of irritation. 'That's Iris Radcliffe. She's a Neighbourhood Watch fanatic.'

'Prompted by taking care of the neighbour's property, or by interest in what goes on over the fence?' he queried softly.

'Mainly the latter, I'm afraid,' Sara said ruefully.

'Shouldn't you be grateful?' he reproved. 'Or are you one of the ungrateful brigade who have no appreciation of neighbourly protection?'

'You've no right to judge me in that manner,' she snapped, her cheeks flushing with indignation. 'You don't know Iris Radcliffe. She's a real gossip.'

'Nor do I wish to know Iris Radcliffe. The lady's curiosity doesn't interest me.' He paused to glare at her. 'What does bother me is my inability to have a rational talk with you.'

Sara became defensive. 'About what?'

'The subject is too lengthy for driveway chatter. Suppose you put your car in the garage while I bring mine into the drive and then perhaps you'll invite me into the house.'

'I'm unlikely to do that.'

He regarded her coldly. 'Miss Masters, you're beginning to bore me. I didn't expect you to be quite so dim.'

'*Dim?* How dare you——?' she began indignantly.

He cut in with sarcasm, 'Anyone with a grain of sense would realise I have a reason for wishing to talk to you.'

She looked at him doubtfully. This man's visit was beyond her comprehension, and she felt a sudden urge to clarify the situation in her own mind. Had Jane really invited him to spend the weekend without mentioning the fact to herself? Had it been an impulse about which the older woman had forgotten? It seemed unlikely.

'Very well, you'd better come in,' she conceded at last.

'Thank you.' His tone was sardonic.

'But don't imagine you'll be staying for long,' she warned him firmly. 'You saw Iris Radcliffe doing sentry duty behind her kitchen curtain. Her tongue is as long as the lake, and she'd love the opportunity to talk about me.'

'You're probably flattering yourself,' he commented in an irritating tone. 'She's sure to have more interesting projects on her mind.'

Sara's lips tightened, but she forbore to snap an angry retort. Instead she led him through the garage and into the house, and as she did so she again became conscious that Leon Longley's appearance was enough to make any girl look twice at him.

But didn't she know all about handsome men? Didn't she know they were the ones to avoid? Terry Purvis had been handsome, she recalled, but thank heavens she had long since evicted him from her system.

Nor was she about to be taken in by the charisma that seemed to emanate from this man. And he needn't imagine that the faint smile hovering about that sensuous mouth would have any effect upon her. She was now immune to all men, wasn't she? Terry had seen to that.

As they reached the living-room Leon Longley stood still to gaze about him, then remarked, 'The cottage is comfortable, even if it is old.'

Sara's brows rose. 'You've seen very little of it, so how would you know whether or not it's comfortable?'

'Perhaps I'll tell you over lunch.' The words came casually.

She was startled. '*Lunch?* What lunch?'

'Perhaps you'll allow me to take you to lunch.'

'No, thank you,' she declined loftily. Did he really think she would place herself under an obligation to him?

'And you've no intention of inviting me to lunch?' he queried as though reading her thoughts. 'I must say I'm becoming rather peckish.'

'Then you'll have to remain peckish,' she retorted.

'But I've come for the weekend,' he pointed out with a hint of determination.

'That's what *you* think.' Sara took a deep breath to control her impatience, then said firmly, 'Let's get this straight. I have no knowledge of any invitation issued to you by my great-aunt. As I've already told you, she's no longer here, so I'm unable to—to extend hospitality to you.'

His expression hardened as he gritted, 'Nevertheless I intend to stay for the weekend, or perhaps even longer—like a week or more if it suits me.'

She was aghast. 'You must be joking!'

'On the contrary, I'm deadly serious.'

A small bubble of fury began to swell within her. 'Then you'd better understand that I have no intention of entertaining a complete stranger—*especially a man*—while living alone in this house. Good grief, you must think I'm out of my mind!'

His eyes glittered with anger as he snarled, 'Do I look as if I'd harm you?'

'Looks can be deceiving,' she snapped. 'Now will you please get out of my home?'

'Not until I've had a cup of tea—even if I have to make it myself.'

'You're absolutely impossible!' she almost shrieked.

'And you're confoundedly inhospitable. I must say I'm mighty disappointed in you. I expected you to be different.'

She looked at him speechlessly, startled by the words that indicated that he had come specially to meet her. They caused her to acquiesce reluctantly. 'Very well, perhaps a cup of tea——'

'And a dry crust?' he pleaded with mock cringing.

'Dry crusts go out to the birds, but there's a stale pizza in the fridge,' she informed him coolly.

'I'm sure it'll be delicious,' he murmured, his eyes hooded.

Sara filled the electric kettle, then placed the pizza in the microwave oven. It had been made only the previous evening from Jane's favourite recipe and was anything but stale, and as she waited for it to heat she deliberately kept her back towards him.

Even so, she knew that he left the room and made his way through the garage towards his car—and she also realised that now was her opportunity to slam and lock the door, yet for some strange reason she lacked the desire to do so. Instead she told herself there was more to this man's visit than met the eye, and she might be wise to learn the motive behind it.

He returned within moments carrying a bottle of wine which he put in the fridge. 'I'm sure you can find glasses?' he queried, raising a brow in her direction.

She complied meekly, placing two stemmed crystal wine glasses on the oak trolley she intended pushing into the living-room.

His next question came silkily. 'By the way, I presume this old cottage still boasts a bathroom?'

She became indignant. 'Of course it does! I suppose you'd like to wash your hands. It's through there——'

'Thank you, I think I can find it.'

Still boasts a bathroom, she thought furiously while setting dishes and the hot pizza on the trolley. *Still——?* Did this mean he had been here before today? Again she suspected there was more to this visit than could be seen on the surface, and she also became aware of a sinking sensation that bore her down, cautioning her that all was not well. Surely the loss of Jane had been enough to contend with—what more was there to come?

Was it possible she was using the wrong tactics with this man? Obviously a constant show of anger was getting her nowhere, so she must humour him. She must tread softly to learn what he had in mind. And then the answer came filtering through as he began to fill their wine glasses.

Raising his own, he said, 'To our future negotiations.'

Sara looked at him blankly. 'Negotiations? I—I'm afraid I don't know what you're talking about.'

He stared into his glass. 'You'll learn, in good time.' Then, almost as though deliberately changing the subject, he observed, 'The garage is quite large. It's wide enough for two cars.'

The words caused her spirits to sink, but she replied calmly, 'At one time it held Samuel's boat, but that space now serves as a woodshed.'

'I'll move the wood by stacking it along the wall.' The statement came casually but held a hint of determination.

Again she was conscious of an icy sensation wrapping itself about her, but she said nothing while cutting the pizza and setting the plate on a small table beside a chair near the window.

'Nice view,' he commented while gazing out towards the lake.

'To the devil with the view!' Sara snapped impatiently. 'Don't you think it's time you told me what all this is about?'

'Surely you can guess?' The question came lazily.

Bewildered, she shook her head. 'I'm afraid not.'

He regarded her patiently while eating the pizza. 'You're sure my name means nothing to you?'

'No, Mr Leon Longley, it does not. If Jane ever mentioned it I've forgotten the occasion. Are you suggesting it's a name that meant something to her?'

'I think you could say it did,' he drawled.

'Then please tell me, where do you fit into Jane's picture?'

'I'm the grandson of Samuel's sister,' he told her.

Her tone became cold while she made no effort to keep the note of disgust from her voice. 'Oh, so you're one of *that* ghastly mob! I might have guessed,' she added, her lip curling in disdain.

His eyes glittered with anger. 'What is *that ghastly mob* supposed to mean?'

'If you knew Jane at all, you'll also be aware of how badly Samuel's relatives treated her. They positively ignored her.'

'I've heard that some of them gave her the cold shoulder.'

'That's a pathetic understatement. They were *beastly* to her! One of them had the temerity to refer to her as an old harpy.' Sara's indignation bubbled as she recalled Jane telling her about Samuel's nieces and nephews. 'I suppose your parents were among those who were so rude to her,' she added bitterly.

Leon Longley's jaw tightened as he rasped with fury, 'You can leave my parents out of the controversy! They both died before Samuel and Jane were married.'

She felt contrite. 'Oh, I'm sorry for suspecting them.'

'But you're right about the others,' he admitted. 'Samuel had two sisters. One was my grandmother, who took control of me when my parents were killed in a car crash.'

'How old were you at that time?' she asked, wondering why she should be interested.

'I was eight—an only child.'

She looked at him in silence, unaware that her hazel eyes betrayed a soft light of compassion as she thought about a small boy losing both parents.

He went on, 'Samuel's other sister also married and had a family. It was her children who had high hopes of inheriting from their uncle's estate, but when he married his housekeeper they were not amused. However, I can't understand their reason for calling her an old harpy. Anyone less like a harpy I've yet to see.'

Sara gave a small shrug. 'It's fairly obvious. A harpy is a greedy person who intends to appropriate everything. One of them even called her a witch, but that was because of her obsession with herbs. The garden is full of them.'

Leon chuckled. 'I recall hearing she was mad about herbs.'

'I think it was the rosemary growing near the front door that set her off, causing her to experiment with other herbs. So many of them have culinary or medicinal uses, so when those nieces or nephews made a rare visit she offered them herbal tea with borage, chives and mint chopped into sandwiches—which they refused.'

'Their preference leaning more towards something out of a bottle,' he commented with a grin.

Sara suppressed a giggle as she recalled Jane's description of the reactions to her herbal offerings.

'Ah, that's better—you almost smiled! You must be feeling more resigned to my presence,' he remarked as a gleam of interest appeared in his eyes.

She looked at him in silence, wondering why his last words had caused another flutter of apprehension, then she admitted, 'At least I'm feeling more at ease now that I know who you are.'

It was true. Her tension had left her, and her curiosity about this man had increased by veering in another direction. Was he married? A man of his appearance would not lack female company for long. Perhaps he was engaged, or on the verge of becoming involved with an attractive woman. Not that it was of any real interest to her, of course.

Her thoughts returned to Jane's in-laws, causing her to say, 'If you'd been among any of those relatives I met I would have remembered you.' Yes, indeed she would have remembered this man, she decided silently, especially that dark auburn hair.

He spoke easily. 'I hadn't seen Jane for years before one day last October when I was driving through the main street of Taupo and happened to see her looking into a shop window. I drove into the nearest parking space, then crossed the road and walked along the pavement to speak to her. She was dressed very smartly in a deep blue woollen suit, and she hadn't a hair out of place.'

'Perhaps she'd just left the salon,' Sara suggested. 'I did her hair every week.'

'I tapped her on the shoulder and said, "Good afternoon, lovely lady—are you looking for an escort to offer you a cup of tea?" She swung round and gaped at me in the most startled manner, her eyes widening into a pair of blue saucers.'

Sara frowned. 'She didn't tell me about this meeting. Are you sure you didn't imagine it?' she demanded sharply.

'My oath, you're a frustrating female!' he gritted. 'I said I was sorry to have startled her, and she said I looked so exactly like Samuel she just couldn't believe it. It seemed I'd given her a shock.'

'Samuel was never far from her mind,' Sara said softly. She was now regretting her former remark.

Leon went on, 'We found a restaurant and chatted mainly about Samuel and my grandmother, and then she wanted me to come and meet you. Or are you still doubtful about all this?'

'I don't know what to think—especially as you didn't come,' Sara reminded him.

'I had to explain that I was on my way from Napier to Auckland, and that I didn't have further time to spare. Several weeks later I received a letter inviting me to spend the weekend—but I've already told you about that.'

'She never mentioned a word about it,' Sara persisted.

'Then I can only say she'd become more forgetful than you realised,' Leon suggested patiently. 'You know how it is with elderly people—they can give you details of the past but can't remember what happened yesterday.'

'Jane wasn't like that,' Sara declared firmly. 'For Pete's sake, I should know. I lived with her!'

'For how long before she died?' The question came casually.

'Four years. I was twenty when I came here after the affair——' She bit off the words, appalled to realise she had been about to say *after the affair with Terry*.

His eyes held a gleam of interest. 'Yes? After what affair?'

'That's not your concern,' she pointed out coldly.

'OK, if it's a dead secret.' Then looking at her appraisingly he said, 'So you're now twenty-four, which makes you eight years my junior.'

She went on hurriedly, 'It was Jane who persuaded me to come to Taupo. Samuel had died and she was living alone. The job in the salon came up when one of the staff married and left to live in the South Island, so Jane spoke to the owner about me filling the girl's place.'

'Which means you were already working at hairdressing?'

'Yes. I began after leaving school. A couple of years later the owner went to Australia and I bought the salon—with Jane's help.'

'And so it became known as Salon Sara.'

'She admitted quite frankly that she thought it would help to keep me with her.' She paused, then said crossly, 'Really, I don't know why I'm telling you about these private matters.'

Leon ignored her outburst by asking, 'Had Jane suffered any illness?'

'Nothing of consequence. She died in her sleep. I took a cup of tea in to her and there she was, peacefully asleep forever. The doctor said it was an aneurysm.' Sara's lids prickled at the memory.

'She couldn't have wished for a better way to go,' he pointed out gently. 'So many people suffer before the end.'

She looked at him thoughtfully, then the question popped out before she could control her tongue. 'Does your wife enjoy good health, Mr Longley?'

He frowned. 'My *wife*? Are you saying I have the look of a careworn married man?'

'Of course not.'

'Then what you're really asking is, am I married?'

'Wrong again,' she snapped, infuriated by her own transparency.

'Then hear this. I am not married, nor am I engaged, nor have I any intention of becoming engaged. I value my freedom too much. But surely *you* have a swain in tow?'

A faint flush had risen to her cheeks. 'Certainly not! I also value my freedom.'

'That's fine,' declared Leon with a hint of satisfaction. 'It will make matters easier in the situation that lies ahead.'

CHAPTER TWO

SARA stared at him blankly. 'Situation, Mr Longley? I'm afraid I don't know what you mean.'

But instead of giving any further explanation he appeared to change the subject by asking a question. 'Am I right in suspecting you haven't been to see John Abernethy since Jane's departure?'

'Yes. I meant to go, but for the entire week we had a rush of work in the salon, so it—it wasn't convenient,' she explained.

'You should have made an appointment to see him at once.' Leon's words held a sharp reprimand. 'He would want to talk to you and to give you a copy of Jane's will, rather than just post it to you.'

Perplexed, she said, 'But I have a fair idea of what her will says. She always told me that—that——' Her words faded into silence, because she had no wish to discuss her inheritance with this man. Even if he did happen to be a great-nephew of Samuel, he was still a stranger to herself, and after all, this was her own private business.

His voice came softly. 'If Abernethy wants to talk to you it's possible her will is not as straightforward as you expect it to be.'

A vague agitation began to rise within her. 'What are you going on about?' Then, throwing discretion to the winds, she admitted, 'Jane always assured me that she intended leaving everything she possessed to me.'

'Which meant——?'

'This cottage, its contents and the income from her shares. Her only stipulation was that the place must be maintained and the herb garden kept in order. She loved the way people came for lavender or sage. People knew that if they wanted parsley or mint it could always be found in Jane's garden. She adored providing these herbs, and perhaps she hoped I'd get the same pleasure.'

'You promised to do these things?' he queried.

'Of course. I shall do my best to carry out Jane's wishes.'

'Maintaining Rosemary Cottage could cost you a lot of money.'

'Then I'll have to bear that cost,' she shrugged. 'Jane bore it, so I suppose I can. I think she'd reached the stage of looking on it as a memorial to Samuel.'

'Old Sam was a sensible fellow. He wouldn't have expected her to do that. He would have advised her to sell the place and move to a maintenance-free flat nearer town.'

Sara shook her head. 'She wouldn't have listened to such advice.'

Leon stared at the toes of his shoes, then asked, 'You don't think she could have had a change of heart since making that will?'

The ominous ring in his words caused her eyes to widen. 'Why would she do that?'

His shoulders lifted in a slight shrug. 'I have a copy of it in the car, so perhaps you'd be wise to take a look at it. I must say it's high time you digested its contents.'

Indignation shook her. 'May I ask how you happen to have a copy of Jane's will? I thought I was the only beneficiary.'

'I have a copy because John Abernethy posted it to me. Excuse me while I fetch it.' His tone had become nonchalant.

Sara felt bewildered as she watched him leave the room, and when he returned the sight of the narrow legal-looking document caused panic to grip her. Something was wrong—she knew it instinctively. Her fingers trembled as she unfolded the pages, then her brain seemed to freeze while her eyes scanned the lines.

A quick glance at the signature swept away any doubt of its being a copy of Jane's will—a new one made only last November. And while her first perusal caused disbelief, the second reading brought on a state of shock as the facts began to register in her mind.

Eventually she understood that while Jane's money and the contents of the cottage had been left to herself, the actual property had been left jointly and in equal shares between her great-niece Sara Annette Masters, and Leon Samuel Longley, great-nephew of her late husband, Samuel Patterson.

Jane had done this to her, after all she had said and promised? *Why*, for heaven's sake? She kept her eyes on the document, refusing to look at the man sitting in the chair opposite. She guessed he was watching for her reaction, and she could almost imagine the sardonic twist of amusement that must be hovering about his lips. The thought caused her to take a firm grip on her control, and if he expected her to go berserk over the situation he would find himself to be mistaken.

At last she sent a cold glance towards Leon Longley. 'What, exactly does this mean?' she queried, making an effort to hide her inner shaking and to keep the tremor from her voice.

'It means that you will not be the sole owner of this property, and that decisions will have to be made. We must study the options.'

'What are the options?' She knew she sounded like a stupid twit and that she should be able to see them for herself, but her mind seemed to have become blank.

'They're simple enough. The property can be sold and the proceeds divided—or you can sell your share to me, or we can both live in it.' His voice held a tinge of amusement.

She was aghast. 'You mean—live in it *together*?'

'Why not?' The question came tersely.

'Because I don't want you here,' Sara declared vehemently. 'I shall not allow you to intrude into my home!'

'*Our* home,' Leon grinned, then spoke seriously. 'You don't appear to have grasped the situation. After probate has been granted I'll no longer be an intruder. I'll be an official part-owner.'

She almost choked with anger. 'Now get this straight— you are not moving into this house. In any case, I thought you said you live in Auckland.'

'The firm's headquarters are in Auckland, but soon there'll be an office in Taupo which I intend to open. While doing so I must have somewhere to live.'

'Well, you're not living *here*!' The words were spat at him.

'My goodness, you do jump up and down!'

'If you imagine you can move in you're very much mistaken!' she snapped furiously, her voice rising to a higher note.

'We'll see about that.' He paused to look at her curiously. 'Tell me, do you blow your top over every small issue?'

'This is not a small issue!' she exclaimed, then curbed her temper as a thought struck her. 'Perhaps you'll agree to sell your share to me. Would that be too much to hope for?'

'Definitely too much, so you can get that idea right out of your head,' rasped Leon with abrupt finality.

Her heart sank as she said, 'I can't understand why you're so interested in this old place.'

'I'm a property developer, remember?' His tone held mockery.

Frustrated, her voice rose to a wail. 'I—I can't believe Jane would do this to me!'

'Well, she did—and no doubt she had her reasons. Perhaps she felt guilty,' he suggested enigmatically.

'*Guilty?* What on earth do you mean? Why should Jane feel guilty? The idea is ridiculous!'

'Not when you think about it. Jane had inherited all she had from Samuel, thereby doing his nieces and nephews out of their expectations from his estate.'

'So what?' Sara demanded indignantly. 'She was his wife, wasn't she? She had a right to inherit his estate.'

'But she knew she couldn't take it with her, so her sense of fairness asserted itself. Instead of leaving what was virtually Samuel's entire estate to her *own* relative, she also included one of *his*. Fortunately, she chose me.'

Sara digested the words until at last she was forced to concede, 'Yes, I see what you mean. That would be typical of Jane—but why would she choose you?'

'Perhaps it was because I never showed antagonism towards her. I agreed with my grandmother that Samuel had been fortunate in finding a caring person to marry him.'

'You weren't full of expectations?' Sara made no attempt to keep the scorn from her voice.

'Why should I bother to convince you on that score? However, for your information, there was no need. I'd already inherited from my parents, and I was in line to inherit from my grandmother. Old Samuel's money meant nothing to me.' Leon paused, looking at her thoughtfully. 'Of course, she could have had another reason for choosing me.'

'Such as?' Her raised brows indicated curiosity.

'Such as the fact that I'd know what to do with the place.'

'Is that so, Mr Property Developer? Haven't I already told you her wishes concerning the property? She wants the cottage maintained and the herb garden kept in order,' Sara reminded him.

'We'll see about that after I've arranged for a thorough examination of the building.'

Apprehension gripped her. 'Are you suggesting something other than maintenance?'

'It's possible,' he admitted casually.

'I—I don't understand,' she faltered.

'It's stupid to spend a fortune on an old cottage that should be replaced,' Leon explained.

'Replaced!' Sara felt shocked. 'Replaced with what?'

'I haven't decided. Holiday units, perhaps. Aren't you aware of the value of this lakeside property?'

Bewildered, she admitted, 'I've never really thought about it.'

'OK, so now's the time to start thinking—and you'd better let me be the judge of the best course to take.'

'But I promised Jane——' she began.

'Jane didn't keep her promise to you. At least, not entirely, so that should free you from feelings of guilt.'

'Nevertheless she's always been very generous to me— and I'm not likely to forget it. Nor shall I forget my promise to her,' Sara asserted firmly.

'That sounds ominous. Does it mean you'll refuse to take my advice and that there'll be constant bickering between us?' His tone had acquired an edge to it.

'Conflict is not what I had in mind. I feel sure we can reach an agreement, if we both remain calm.'

Leon chuckled. 'Kindly remember that I'm not the one who's been flying up in the air.' Then a gleam of interest appeared in the brown eyes as he said, 'What sort of agreement have you in mind? I've already pointed out the options.'

'Then let me ask you again—would you be willing to sell your share of the property to me?'

'And I can only repeat *definitely not*—and that it would be more to the point for you to sell your half to me.'

'No, no——!' The words were wrenched from her like a cry of pain. 'I love this cottage. It's full of memories for me. It was a place of refuge when—when——' The words died on her lips.

'Yes——? When——?' The query came softly.

'Must I ask you to mind your own business?' she demanded coldly.

Unperturbed, he continued to probe. 'Was it when you had an unhappy love affair? Is that why you went to live with Jane?'

'Will you *shut up* about my private affairs!' Sara retorted through tight lips. His guess had been so definitely on target she was unable to meet his eyes, and she turned away to gaze across the lake.

'OK, I'll do that,' he grinned. 'In the meantime I'll fetch my bag from the car.'

His words sent her into a further jittery state she was unable to control, and, following him to the door she shouted at his receding back, 'You can get into your car and drive away. I mean it—*please go away*!'

The sound of his laugh reached her ears.

Infuriated, she slammed the door, locked it, then pulled down the kitchen blinds and drew the curtains across the living-room windows. No way would she have him peering at her through the glass, she decided, huddling in a chair and hoping to hear his car leave.

But the purr of the Daimler's departure did not reach her ears. Instead the peal of the front doorbell shrilled through the cottage, the sound making her nerves jump although she remained crouched in the chair.

The bell pealed again, echoing through the rooms with an imperative demand to be answered. There was another brief pause, then Sara was brought to her feet with a bound as she heard the front door open. Moments later she watched Leon carry a suitcase into the living-room while still dangling a small object from his other hand.

Her eyes widened at the sight of it. 'You have a key!' she exclaimed incredulously.

He examined it gravely. 'Is *that* what it is? I wondered how it opened the door so easily.'

'Wh-where did you get it?' she demanded, unable to conceal the bewildered state of her mind.

'John Abernethy sent it to me with the copy of the will,' he informed her in an offhand manner. 'Appar-

ently Jane left it with him, and with instructions to do
so.'

Sara could only stare at him in frustrated silence, her
mind endeavouring to cope with the situation. But no
matter which way her thoughts darted they returned to
one salient fact. *He had a key to her house.* He could
walk in and out of it whenever he pleased. As she thought
about it, her face mirrored her dismay.

Watching her narrowly Leon commented in a dry tone,
'I believe the picture is becoming clear to you at last.'

Unable to speak, she nodded miserably.

'Good. Then perhaps you'll show me where I'm to
sleep.' The words were spoken politely, yet they came in
the form of a command which seemed to hammer home
the fact that he had moved in.

Sara took a grip on herself, remaining calm only with
difficulty. 'You'd better come this way,' she said, feeling
defeated.

She led him from the living-room to the passage, where
she paused beside a closed door. 'This front room was
Jane's bedroom. I haven't done anything about it yet,
so it's just as she left it. While it's untouched I feel that—
that she isn't so far away.'

'I understand,' he said with surprising gentleness.

'Next to it is the bathroom, and then comes my room.'
Opening the door of the third bedroom, she went on,
'This is the guest-room. The bed is already made, but
you'll need towels.' She went to the linen cupboard,
which was also in the passage, and extracted two large
fluffy towels which she carried to the bathroom and hung
over a rail, her actions automatic despite her sense of
shock.

Following her, Leon made an obvious attempt to be
friendly. 'Did you ever meet my great-uncle Samuel?'
he queried in a conversational tone.

'Only once, when they visited my grandmother. Gran
and Jane were sisters. At the time I was little more than
a child, and to me he seemed to be a very old man. He

was bent and needed help from Jane because of his arthritis. I can assure you she took great care of him,' Sara added pointedly while endeavouring to remain calm.

She left him abruptly and went to her own room, where she shut the door. Leaning her back against it, she closed her eyes, feeling shaken by this unexpected turn of events, especially as a mere two hours ago she had believed that this was her own home, left to her by Jane. But the sudden intrusion of the man in the guest-room had shattered that delusion.

Her thoughts flew to Mr Abernethy, and she recalled his look of concern when he had spoken to her at the funeral. At the time she had attributed his morose attitude to the sombre occasion, but she now realised he'd known of this state of affairs. *Of course* he'd known— he'd drawn up the will, hadn't he?

'Come and see me as soon as possible,' he had requested. 'It's important. Mrs Patterson would wish you to do so.'

But had she gone to him? No. If she had done so she would have been warned about this bombshell. She would have been ready to catch it with both hands— instead of which she'd allowed it to explode at her feet. 'OK, Mr Abernethy,' she muttered audibly to herself. 'I'll see you first thing on Monday morning—*my oath, I will*! Perhaps you'll be able to tell me what put this idea into Jane's head. No doubt she had a reason, and I'd like to be able to understand it.'

She remembered that the lunch dishes were waiting to be washed, but when she reached the kitchen she discovered Leon putting the last of them away. 'There's no need——' she began.

'I intend to do my share of the chores,' he informed her gravely, then paused to stare at the woodwork above the cupboard door.

'Something's wrong?' she queried, following his narrowed gaze.

'I'm wondering if that's a borer hole up there. Old timber houses are inclined to become infested by borer.'

Her irritation bubbled. 'Are you suggesting that this one is standing only because the borer grubs are holding hands? It might interest you to learn that Jane had the cottage treated. We had to get out while it was being done.'

'Perhaps they've returned with their friends and relations.'

She faced him angrily. 'Why does it please you to condemn this place?' she demanded.

'Because something better could be built on the site, especially if it's riddled with borer.'

'Ah, Mr Property Developer speaks up loud and clear,' she said with derision.

'Prompted by Mr Common Sense,' he retorted.

She sent him a direct glare. 'Please understand there's only one species of *borer* concerning me at the moment.'

His lips twitched. 'Don't tell me—let me guess.'

'It shouldn't be difficult,' she snapped. 'The fact that you own half this house doesn't mean you have to live in it.'

'You don't think it could have been what Jane had in mind?' The question was accompanied by a faint smile.

'Certainly not—it's the *last* thing she'd have in mind. Jane had very strict standards, and not for one moment would she expect me to be compromised. I suppose you *do* realise that you *are* compromising me?' Sara quavered.

'I am? I didn't think it mattered in this day and age.'

'Of course it matters!' she almost shrieked. 'Heaven alone knows what the neighbours will be saying. The thought of their wagging tongues gives me the horrors. Iris Radcliffe will tell the world that it hasn't taken long for me to get a man into the house.'

'Your fears are groundless, nor is there any need to work yourself into a state of such agitation. I'll assure them that our relationship is purely platonic—and that where I'm concerned you'll be as safe as if you were in church.'

The words needled her. 'How do you propose to achieve that miracle?' she demanded coldly.

'Simply by telling them that girls with eyes continually flashing yellow sparks of anger have no appeal for me,' he returned blandly. *'No appeal whatever,'* he emphasised.

Her expression changed to one of resentment which concealed an underlying hurt. Was this his subtle way of telling her she was unattractive? She knew her face with its retroussé nose hadn't carried her many rungs up the beauty ladder, but Jane had always assured her that she had a pleasing personality, and that it was the way a person *thought* that mattered.

Her chin held a shade higher, she said, 'Your opinion of my appearance is not important, Mr Longley. Nor have I any intention of pretending you could become a welcome companion in this house.'

'No?' His tone was mocking. 'No doubt the reverse will be the case—your main object being to get me out of the house.' He sent her an irritating grin. 'Well, I'm afraid you'll not find that an easy task.'

Nor was it long before Sara realised the truth of his words, because within a short time he became busy in the garage, where the scattered wood was taking up half the space.

'Just making room for my car,' he explained, opening the double doors. 'My half of the garage, you understand?'

She watched him stacking the small logs against the wall, and as he bent to the task she became conscious of muscles rippling beneath the fawn trousers and tan shirt. The short sleeves of the latter revealed dark hairs on his arms, while the open neck displayed a triangle of crisp dark hairs. Already he's very much at home, she thought, dragging her eyes away from the broad

shoulders and slim hips, and at the same time becoming
conscious of his vitality.

Something about his aura of masculinity disturbed her,
causing her to turn away with the intention of going
inside the cottage. And then his voice made her pause.
'We have a visitor,' he said. 'Neighbourhood Watch has
come for a closer view.'

Sara turned again, this time to see Iris Radcliffe entering the drive, and she had no option but to go forward
and meet her.

Iris was a small thin woman with a tight mouth which
now smiled effusively as she almost cooed, 'Sara dear,
could you spare a few sprigs of parsley?' And although
she spoke to Sara her sharp pale blue eyes were taking
in every detail of Leon Longley's handsome appearance.

Sara became conscious of a sinking feeling as she
realised that Iris Radcliffe had begun checking the situation at once. However, she managed to smile as she
said, 'Of course—it's over here. Pick as much as you
want.'

But the neighbour did not move. Instead she stood
waiting to be introduced to Leon.

An imp urged Sara to leave her standing there, and
as she bent to pick the parsley she heard Iris attempt to
make conversation. 'The garage is quite spacious when
the wood has been stacked,' were the words that came
to her ears.

'Yes.' Leon's reply came abruptly.

'Dear Jane, we'll all miss her. You knew her well, Mr—
er——?'

Sara smiled to herself as she imagined Iris Radcliffe's
brows raised in silent question, but although she strained
her ears for Leon's answer, none came as he continued
to stack the wood. She snatched a few more stems of
the curly green herb, and as she rejoined them the
neighbour turned to her expectantly, her eyes alive with
interest as she waited for an introduction.

However, it was forestalled as Leon moved from them to grasp a yard broom. 'I'm about to make the dust fly,' he warned. Nor did he exaggerate, and within moments the rising cloud had caused Sara and Iris to make hasty exits from the garage.

'Who is that man?' the latter demanded crossly.

'Just a—a distant relative,' Sara explained evasively.

'A relative? I don't recall seeing him before today—and I see most things from my kitchen window.'

'I'm sure you do, Mrs Radcliffe,' Sara returned drily.

'He had no need to begin sweeping at that precise moment, just as you were about to introduce him to me.' Iris's tone was aggrieved while her expression betrayed resentment as she added, 'I can't help feeling his action was deliberate.'

'Oh, no, it wouldn't have been deliberate, Mrs Radcliffe,' Sara said quickly, then bit off her words, amazed to find herself defending Leon Longley.

The neighbour's voice took on an ominous note. 'Perhaps I should tell you I saw him arrive during the morning while you were at work. I watched him walk round the house as though examining the place, and I saw him staring at the windows. I even contemplated ringing the police.'

Sara chuckled inwardly. 'Why didn't you, Mrs Radcliffe?'

'Well, he looked so *respectable* and not at all like an *ordinary* burglar, especially with that car.'

'What does an ordinary burglar look like? Somebody wearing a mask and with a sack slung over his shoulder?'

Iris refused to be amused. 'There's nothing funny about burglars. When this man disappeared I began to fear he'd really broken into the house.'

'As it happens, he has his own key.' Sara felt compelled to admit to this fact, knowing that sooner or later it would become obvious.

'Really?' More interest sparked from the pale blue eyes that swept a sharp glance over Sara, then enlightenment appeared to dawn as Iris queried, 'He's come to *stay*? Is that why he's clearing a space in the garage?'

'Jane had invited him for a weekend, before she died,' Sara explained, at the same time fearing that a mere weekend would be too much to hope for. 'But thank you for your concern.'

'Neighbourhood Watch,' Iris reminded her virtuously, her mouth tightening as she added, 'But, my dear, you must be careful.'

Sara's brows rose. 'Careful, Mrs Radcliffe?'

Iris sent a swift glance towards the garage. 'That man—after all, *he is a man.*'

'Yes, I've noticed. So what?'

Iris licked her thin lips. 'Well, you know *men*—or perhaps it's as Jane said, and you *don't* know men.'

Sara felt a surge of indignation. 'What do you mean?'

'Jane said you seldom go out with men, and that means you could be vulnerable. If that man turns on the charm—and he probably has plenty—he could get you into bed in a trice.'

'Indeed he could *not*!' Sara snapped haughtily.

'Believe me, you could become like putty in his hands.'

'I'll buckle on my chastity belt,' Sara promised, making an effort to curb her rising anger.

'On top of *that*, my dear, there's the matter of what people will *say*.' Iris sent glances from left to right as though expecting to see members of the local community trooping along the road in a body.

Sara took a firm grip on her patience. She was becoming weary of Iris Radcliffe's insinuations, and, forcing a smile, she said, 'Please help yourself to any other herbs you need. It's what Jane would have wished.' She returned to the garage, where the dust had subsided.

Leon grinned at her. 'Interested, was she?'

'You can say that again!' Sara's retort bubbled with anger.

'Why be so uptight? You should be grateful to a neighbour who keeps an eye on your property, even if it does mean your movements being reported far and wide.'

'They don't normally include men with their own key,' she said coldly.

'You told her I have a key? Wasn't that rather indiscreet?'

She sent him a withering glare. 'She'd watched you arrive before I came home. She thought you'd got into the house in some way, and as she'll soon know you've taken up residence there seemed to be little point in keeping it from her.' Her last words were filled with reproach.

'Yes, I suppose she might as well know I've reserved a bed in the cottage.'

Frustrated, she almost stamped her foot. 'I do think you're being most inconsiderate! You could easily find somewhere else to live. Believe me, Jane wouldn't like it.'

'How can you be so sure of that?' Leon queried.

'Because I knew Jane. She had very old-fashioned ideas.'

'Didn't you know she lived with Samuel before they were married?'

'That was different. It was her job. She was his housekeeper,' Sara pointed out.

Leon laughed. 'I can't see that that makes any difference. They were living together—and no doubt sleeping together.'

Sara drew a sharp breath. 'That's absurd! They were so much older, and I don't believe——'

'You're suggesting they were—past it? You must be naïve if you imagine sex stops at middle age.'

Her cheeks had become flushed. 'I'm not in the habit of dwelling on sex,' she informed him loftily, her retroussé nose slightly in the air.

'Are you admitting to the fact that you're frigid?'

'Certainly not!'

He stepped closer to her, staring down into her face while he eyed her narrowly. 'Perhaps you've had a jolt at some time. You've been hurt. Somebody has switched you off, causing you to become anti-male.'

His words shocked her because they were so near the truth. 'You don't know what you're talking about,' she hedged in a low voice.

'Don't I? Your attitude towards me speaks volumes,' he accused relentlessly. 'Normally I have no difficulty in my association with members of the opposite sex, but you—you're the proverbial ice maiden.'

'While you consider yourself God's gift to women,' she retaliated, making an effort to control her rising exasperation. 'Tell me, do these women who melt at your touch arrive home to discover you've intruded into their own private domains?'

His jaw tightened while his tone became sardonic. 'Isn't it time you made an attempt to remember I own half this particular domain?'

She wilted visibly. 'Yes, I'm having difficulty in becoming accustomed to the idea. I was a fool not to have gone to—to the solicitor at once.'

'And then you could have awaited my arrival with bated breath,' he almost snarled. 'You could have stood behind the door with an axe in your hand. You'd have enjoyed that——'

'Thank you for your high opinion of me,' she cut in furiously. 'First I'm as cold as ice, and now I'm a potential murderess! Is there any other title you'd like to hang on me?'

'I'll have to think about it.'

'Can't you understand that the week has been bad enough without all this extra hassle?' She paused, then flashed at him, 'Iris Radcliffe wasn't far wrong when she thought you were an intruder.'

'I'll admit I came earlier and walked round the house. Was that so terrible, considering the circumstances?' he queried.

'It was only the sight of your car that made her think you could be a respectable person.' She turned to look at the expensive white Daimler parked in the drive. Did its quality reflect its owner, or did it merely give an impression of prosperity to the world?

Leon chuckled. 'That proves that all burglars should drive a good car. I must tell any I happen to meet.'

Sara refused to be amused, and as she went indoors she flung at him, 'You know perfectly well you could have booked into a motel instead of deciding to push in here!'

He followed her to the living-room, where he found her staring moodily through the front window. Standing behind her, he gritted in a low voice, 'Even you must realise it's the height of the season. Thousands of people come to Taupo on holiday at this time of the year, especially with the school holidays being in full force—so you should be ready to concede that the hotels and motels could be fully booked out.'

'Yes, I—I suppose so,' she admitted reluctantly, knowing this to be a fact.

His voice was still hard. 'In that case, it might interest you to learn that I tried to find alternative accommodation, but was unable to do so. So I was forced to avail myself of Jane's invitation, especially as John Abernethy had already sent me the key she'd left in his care.'

Sara did not miss the irony in his voice. 'I'll be on his doorstep first thing Monday morning,' she assured him, her voice ringing with determination.

'No doubt his advice will be similar to the wisdom he handed to me,' Leon remarked drily.

'Oh? And that was——?'

'Mutual agreement appears to be the only solution to the situation. We must both agree to the outcome of the property, and while we're working on that project we should be searching for a little more agreement between ourselves. Otherwise we'll get precisely nowhere.'

CHAPTER THREE

SARA had not previously heard such a ring of authority in Leon's voice. It seemed to echo his intention to dominate the situation, and she was immediately put on her guard. No way would he be allowed to boss her, she decided.

At the same time she realised he was right, and having digested the wisdom of his words she turned to face him. 'I can understand that we must find mutual agreement,' she admitted reluctantly. 'However, I fail to see why it's necessary for us to live under the same roof while doing so.'

'Obviously, you don't want me here,' he rasped.

'I thought I'd made myself perfectly clear on that point. As you know, there'll be a period before probate is granted, so why don't you return to Auckland until after that date?'

'Because I've no intention of doing so,' he informed her coldly. 'You appear to be forgetting I'm in Taupo to open a branch office. Perhaps you'd prefer that I slept under the stars while attending to it?'

Sara could find no reply.

His brows drew together as he stared down into her face. 'The opinions of the neighbours worry you to such an extent?' he demanded tersely. 'Or do you fear repercussions of a different nature?'

The question startled her. 'What do you mean?'

His eyes narrowed as he regarded her intently. 'Is there a man who'll object to my presence in the house?' he demanded bluntly.

She turned back to the window while wondering what answer to give. Since the unfortunate affair with Terry Purvis she had been wary of establishing a definite re-

40

lationship with any of the men who had sought her company, but now she found herself loath to admit she did not have a special boyfriend. It made her appear to be unattractive to the male sex, and the thought caused pride to raise its head.

Avoiding his glance, she said frostily, 'Believe it or not, I *do* get taken out by the opposite sex—but how shall I explain your presence in the house? What are they going to think?'

'Surely not the worst?' he teased, grinning broadly.

'You appear to find the situation hilarious,' she snapped furiously. 'Let me tell you I'm not amused by your intrusion into my social life.'

'No?' Leon frowned thoughtfully. 'In that case, we'll have to see what can be done about it.'

Her spirits lifted as a sudden hope dawned. 'You mean you'll go away? You'll go home to Auckland after all—or have you something else in mind?'

'A chaperon. You need another woman in the house. Someone to stop the wagging tongues of the neighbours, and to still the suspicions of your boyfriends. We mustn't allow them to think I'm entering your bed every night.'

Sara's cheeks reddened as she gasped, 'That's most unlikely to happen. You'll not crawl into my bed——'

'You're right—I never crawl. I usually stride in and fling back the bedclothes while the maiden utters wild cries of ecstatic anticipation.'

She regarded him seriously. 'The striding in part I can well believe. After all, when it comes to *intruding*, what's a mere bedroom when compared to an entire house? But thank you for warning me to keep my door locked.'

'You're saying there'd be no cries of ecstasy?'

'None whatever,' she retorted vehemently. 'There'd be only shouts that could reach the neighbours. Iris Radcliffe, her husband and son would be here in a flash.'

'Then you agree that a chaperon could be the answer?' The question came casually.

'Yes, I suppose you're right,' she admitted, conscious of feeling a definite lack of enthusiasm towards the idea.

'Ah, we progress. We actually agree on one point.' Then his tone became brisk as he queried, 'Is it possible you know of a suitable woman who could come and live with us?'

'You mean someone older than myself?'

'I mean someone who will allay suspicion that I'm sleeping with you every night,' Leon explained.

Sara caught her breath as the thought of sleeping with him every night sent quivers shooting through her nerves, then she shook her head, while forcing her mind to rake through the list of older women she had met through Jane. There seemed to be no one, and at last she said, 'I can't think of a single person. Perhaps we should advertise—or perhaps I should consult Mrs Radcliffe. She might know of a suitable woman.'

'I doubt that it'll be necessary to bring her into the picture—or even to advertise,' Leon added as an afterthought.

'Are you saying you know of someone?'

'It's possible. As it happens, I have a friend who *might* come until we get the fate of Rosemary Cottage sorted out.'

'*Fate?*' The word startled her. 'That sounds ominous—almost as though you really could consider pulling it down.'

'I haven't yet made up my mind,' he told her with a hint of his hidden dominance creeping into his voice.

Sara glared at him. '*Your* mind?' she exclaimed. 'What about *my* mind? Isn't my opinion also to be considered?'

'As I've already explained, your mind and my mind must merge in agreement.'

She became angry, her voice rising as she turned away from him and flung herself on the settee. 'I shall never agree to this house being pulled down, so you'd better get that straight in your mind here and now. I promised Jane, and that's all there is to it.'

Leon shrugged, his manner one of extreme boredom as he sat in the chair near the window. 'Must we go over all that again?' he drawled. 'Personally, I'd prefer to concentrate on the establishment of our compatibility.'

Sara's eyes narrowed to conceal the sparks of suspicion she feared could be lurking within their depths. She resented the sight of him lounging in Jane's favourite chair, his long legs stretched before him, his relaxed attitude giving the impression that he had already acquired the property. Frustrated, she exclaimed in a tight voice, '*Compatibility*—how do you propose to bring about that miracle?'

'By forgetting the cottage for a while. We could go for a drive. I haven't seen Huka Falls for years. I believe a village of some sort has been established in the vicinity.'

'Yes, it's known as Huka Village. It's a tourist attraction with early-settlement-type shops and cottages. There's a blacksmith's forge and livery stables.'

'So you can take me on a guided tour. We can get to know each other.'

Sara hesitated, conscious of her mind being dragged in opposite directions. If she complied with his request it would indicate that she was ready to fall in with whatever suggestion he saw fit to put forward, and she had no intention of doing that. But if she refused it would delay the opportunity of reaching an amicable agreement—one which could possibly veer towards Jane's wishes.

Leon sensed her hesitation. 'You feel reluctant to come out with me? Believe me, you'll be quite safe. I've no intention of tossing you over the falls, especially with dozens of tourists looking on.'

The words made her feel defiant. Did he imagine she was afraid of him? Nor did she intend to respond to his levity, so she merely said, 'Very well, I'll come. Just give me five minutes.'

'Right. I'll see that the doors are locked.'

The remark, offered with a grin, made her suspect he
was laughing at her, but she decided to ignore it as she
hurried to her bedroom, where she changed into a
gathered floral skirt with a wide belt and cream blouse.
Her make-up was attended to, and as she smoothed extra
colour on to her soft, generous mouth she began to
wonder why she was taking this special care with her
face.

'Don't I always do my best with my face—such as it
is?' she mumbled at her reflection in the mirror. 'It has
nothing to do with the fact that I'm going out with *him*.
Definitely nothing at all.'

Later, as she sat beside him in the white Daimler, she
felt herself being gripped by a feeling of unreality. The
situation was becoming completely ridiculous, especially as she was now being wafted into a state of
relaxation that was difficult to discard. She should be
uptight. She should be keeping a firm hold on her state
of righteous indignation, but somehow it seemed to be
slipping away from her.

Searching for the reason, she blamed the tranquillity
of the scene. The placid blue waters dotted with brightly
coloured sails, the people basking on the white pumice
beach, the distant mountains—somehow it all spoke of
peace.

The route turned to take them through the Taupo
shopping area, then crossed the bridge where the Waikato
River left the lake to rush between narrow gorges before
finding its way to the sea. A short distance took them
to the Huka Road on which they found the historic
village, and then the ring of the hammer drew them towards the blacksmith's forge.

As they watched the man in his leather apron Leon
spoke in Sara's ear. 'He represents a much slower life-
style, perhaps with fewer problems than our own.'

Memory caused her to say, 'Jane always declared we
should live each day as if we thought it was to be our
last.'

He shot an oblique glance at her. 'I'm surprised you don't follow her advice.'

She felt needled. 'What do you mean?' she demanded.

'You could make an effort to shake off that resentment you're holding against me. It sticks out a mile.'

Her anger surged back to reassert itself. 'That surprises you, when I've just lost my home? You could make an effort to understand that I'm very upset. Or is that too much to expect of you?'

'And you could make a further effort to remember I didn't tell Jane what to put in her will. At least I'll try to do what I consider she'd want me to do.'

'Naturally—it'll mean my loss being your gain.' The words were flung at him with a bitterness that echoed in her own ears.

'This attitude you're so determined to hold does nothing to help matters,' he rasped. 'But then I doubt if you *want* to help matters.'

Sara made no reply as they left the village and made their way further along the road to where the river was spanned by a short bridge stretching across a narrow rock-walled passage. Pausing on it, they stared down at the turbulence of seething rapids that sped along the chasm towards the Huka Falls.

The sight always made Sara feel nervous. 'Nobody would have a chance in that lot,' she remarked above the noise of the liquid insanity below them.

Leon's fingers took a firm grip on her arm. 'My intrusion into your life causes you to contemplate jumping over?'

She snatched her arm away. 'You flatter yourself,' she scoffed.

'Nevertheless we'll move off the bridge before you're hypnotised into doing something stupid. Believe me, I've no intention of going down there to fish you out.'

'I'll bet you haven't!' Her retort oozed bitterness.

His eyes rested on her face in a long and penetrating scrutiny. 'So much for reaching a mutual agreement,' he gritted icily. 'You have no intention of making the slightest attempt to do so. Really, Sara, I'm becoming somewhat bored with you, and with your constant antagonism.'

His words came like a slap in the face, making it impossible for her to find a suitable reply.

He went on relentlessly, 'You must have had Jane completely fooled. She must have been as blind as a hen in the dark.'

She was startled. 'Jane? What do you mean?'

'When she wrote inviting me to visit for a weekend she said I'd be interested in meeting her great-niece whom, she felt sure, I'd discover to be good company.'

'Jane said that?' Despite herself Sara felt pleased.

'Indeed she did. But she was mistaken. From her description of you I expected to find a sweet girl with a pleasing personality. Sadly I've failed to do so,' he told her through tight lips.

Pride caused her chin to rise as the statement hit her like a douche of icy water. 'So what have you found?' she demanded with angry defiance.

'Someone who's completely self-centred and wrapped up in her own woes. To be honest, you're a pain in the neck.'

She gave a small gasp of fury. 'Thank you very much! But even you must admit I have reason——'

He cut in, 'You've been plunged into a situation you don't like, and instead of coping with it in a sane manner you're allowing it to churn you into a frenzy of ill temper. Inside yourself you're exactly like those raging waters down there.'

'You're exaggerating,' she accused in an aloof manner.

'Not at all. And there's something else I'd like to point out.'

'You have further fault to find with me?' she queried in the most scathing tone she could muster.

'Apparently you haven't yet learned that it's the unexpected that leaps up to change the course of one's entire life.'

A shrill laugh escaped her. 'You dare to suggest *that*—after the unexpected that leapt at me today?'

'Then allow me to show you something,' said Leon.

They left the bridge and made their way along the track. On their right the scrubby hillside was dotted by clumps of native pampas grass, the long-stemmed creamy plumes rising like ostrich feathers above the surrounding darker foliage. On their left protective railing bordered the drop to the river, and as they stood at one of the fenced viewpoints Leon bent his head to speak in her ear.

'The falls are not spectacular for height,' he said. 'It's the force of their brutal power and their extreme foaming that makes them remain in the memory.'

Sara, conscious of his hand on her shoulder, tried to ignore its pressure as she said, 'That's what you wanted to show me?'

He continued to gaze across the intervening space towards the outlet of the rock-walled chasm. 'Yes. We were speaking of the unexpected. Those madly seething waters in the narrow passageway know nothing of what lies ahead. They struggle and fight until suddenly they positively explode through the opening, which is a gap of only a few yards wide.'

She turned to stare downstream. 'But within a few minutes they become tranquil because the river has widened. I love its unusual pale blue-green colour.'

'That's what I wanted to impress on you,' Leon explained.

'The—the blue-green colour?' The pressure of his fingers had become more intense, making it difficult for her to think clearly.

'No—the tranquillity. The calm after the storm. The settling down to a normal flow after the unexpectedness of being hurtled along.' He turned to look at her. 'You also will settle down to a new state of affairs, if only you'll give yourself the chance to do so.'

'Instead of being a constant pain in the neck?' Sara flashed at him resentfully.

'I couldn't have put it better myself,' he commented.

'Thank you,' she retorted, irritated by his frankness, and by the fact that he made no attempt to conceal his poor opinion of her. Strangely, it made her feel depressed, causing her to turn and walk away from him.

His long strides caught up with her. 'Don't run away, the drive isn't yet over—unless you feel like walking home.'

She turned to face him, her expression bleak. 'I would if it weren't so far,' she told him quietly.

They returned to where the Daimler had been left, and as she took her seat in it Sara felt invaded by an overwhelming weariness. She guessed it had been caused by her own inner turmoil of anger, and she realised that this was something she would be wise to shake off, so she raked her mind for words that would keep the conversation on neutral ground. However, all she could say was, 'This is a very comfortable car.'

'Yes. I inherited it from my grandmother—Granny Grace, I used to call her. She was the one who took me under her wing when I lost my parents. I was her sole heir.'

'And your grandfather—has he also—gone?' she asked, conscious of the surge of interest in these matters that were his affairs and of no concern to herself. Yet, strangely, she was keen to learn more about his background.

'Yes, he died several years before Granny Grace. He was also a property developer. He urged me to join the company he'd formed twenty years previously, his plea being that if he couldn't have his son with him, he'd at least have his grandson.'

'So you're alone?' asked Sara, still making no effort to curb her curiosity.

'Not exactly. I have numerous friends,' Leon admitted casually.

'One of them being the woman who'll come to stay with us?' she asked, eager to learn more about this person.

'That's right. I doubt if she'll refuse to come—unless it's not possible for her to do so at the moment.'

'Is she someone your grandmother knew?' She put the question in an offhand manner while still searching for more information.

'Of course. She's been a family friend for years.'

Somebody middle-aged, Sara decided. Somebody—she hoped—who would attend to Leon's meals and laundry, because if he imagined that she herself would be tied to these chores he could think again. Problems lay ahead, instinct whispered, then common sense told her to face them when they arose.

Deep in thought, she was hardly aware they had reached Wairakei until the car slackened speed to turn and purr its way between the shaven lawns and colourful flowerbeds of the Wairakei Hotel. The sprawling complex was noted for its facilities for large conferences, and when Leon stopped at the main entrance Sara sent him a glance of enquiry. Was he about to make a further request for accommodation? she wondered hopefully.

However, he made no comment as he left the car and disappeared into the foyer. When he returned minutes later he merely said, 'We'll be having dinner here this evening.'

A sharp intake of breath betrayed her indignation. 'But you didn't ask me,' she protested.

His brows rose. 'I didn't consider it to be necessary.'

She became agitated. '*You* didn't consider——? Who do you think you are?' she stormed. 'I refuse to be taken for granted in this high-handed manner! What makes you so sure I haven't other arrangements for this evening?'

'If you have, Tom, Dick, Harry or whoever will have to be put off. You can tell him it's Leon's turn, and that you have other fish to fry.'

She began to feel hysterical. 'You've got a nerve!'

Leon remained unmoved, then grinned as he went on, 'You can tell *whoever* that Jane threw a beautiful big trout right into your lap and that you must learn to handle it.'

'Beautiful? Huh! You certainly are as slippery as a trout—and you sure need stripping down to your last scale,' she told him wrathfully.

He was silent for several moments, then turned to regard her with a thoughtful frown on his brow. 'Did you have plans for this evening?' he queried.

'To be honest, I didn't. But that's not the point.'

Leon's mouth tightened. 'The point being that you have no intention of budging one inch towards a compatible relationship. OK, I'll admit I should have asked, but I turned in at the entrance on impulse and reserved a table before giving it a second thought. However, it's not important. When we get home I'll phone and cancel it.'

Sara looked down to where her hands rested in her lap. She was being a fool, she decided. Her constant anger against him must be controlled, because her attitude was doing nothing towards a state of agreement concerning the cottage. And while Leon was doing his part by holding out the hand of friendship, she was refusing to reach out and grasp it.

At last she said in a small voice that still betrayed reluctance, 'Very well, I suppose I'll come.'

'You'll actually condescend to do so?' His tone was sardonic. 'I must say that's mighty big of you.'

Little more was said until they reached home, and then Sara's curiosity was stirred when she saw Leon spread a map on the kitchen table. At first she tried to ignore it, but eventually she found herself drawing near to give it closer examination.

'It's a map showing how the land round the lake is being used,' he explained, moving his finger across the paper. 'These sections are forest reserve, and here we have areas for development.'

'No doubt they're the ones that interest you.' Her tone was ironical.

'Naturally. Tomorrow I'll take a drive to examine them.' He paused, then invited casually, 'Would you care to come with me? We could picnic beside the lake with a few sandwiches and a thermos of tea.'

'No, thank you. The household chores must be done at weekends. Besides, I'm sure this evening will be sufficient for you to suffer a—a pain in the neck such as myself.'

An exclamation of impatience escaped him as he swung round to face her. His hands gripped her shoulders to give her a severe shake, and as he glared down at her he snarled, 'Must you belabour the point? I'm beginning to suspect you're revelling in your own bitchiness!'

Sara wrenched herself free, her cheeks scarlet as her eyes flashed sparks of anger. 'Don't you dare lay your hands on me—and you might as well know I *do* feel *thoroughly* bitchy. Deep down I'm positively hopping mad with this entire situation, and if you imagine a picnic beside the lake or a dinner at the Wairakei will wipe it away you're very much mistaken!'

His expression became thunderous. 'OK, I've got the message,' he rasped. 'It's a pity Jane can't get it as well. I doubt if she'd be amused. She'd probably remind you that she'd already been generous to you, and that the house was hers to leave as she pleased. However, she was probably unaware of your greed,' he finished icily.

His words left her feeling stricken, not only because she sensed a certain amount of truth in them, but also because they revealed that he held her in contempt. And now it was only pride that enabled her to say, 'You seem to be forgetting that Jane *promised*——'

'Something to which she gave a lot more thought,' he finished for her. 'And incidentally, isn't it time you switched your own thoughts to something more pleasant?'

'Like what?' she demanded wearily.

'Like dressing up to go out this evening,' he grinned.

'Never in my life have I felt less like dressing up—especially to go out with a man who holds such a low opinion of me.'

'Then why not shake off your misery and make an attempt to raise that opinion?' Leon suggested silkily.

'Because *your* opinion means nothing to me,' she informed him sharply, her chin tilted at a higher angle.

'My goodness, you are a mass of contradictions! You've got me all confused,' he mocked, then turned his back on her while he continued to study the map.

Her eyes rested on the auburn lights in his dark hair while she muttered beneath her breath, 'And you've got me completely confused, you devastating devil!' Then she went to her room, where she flung herself on the bed.

For a time she lay simmering in a cauldron of grievances, but eventually her disgruntled mood subsided sufficiently for her thoughts to veer towards what she would wear. Colour was needed—something to lift her from out of the gloom—and when she emerged from her room at seven o'clock she was wearing a pure silk skirt and top that rivalled the rainbow.

Admiration flashed into Leon's eyes as she walked into the living-room. 'That dress is really quite stunning,' he remarked quietly.

The dress, not me, Sara thought bleakly, but managed a faint smile as she said, 'Thank you.'

'And that smile adds to the effect,' he commented. 'I'm wondering if it betrays a pleasing personality that's been kept under lock and key all day. I trust it'll be let loose for the rest of the evening.'

'Today I haven't felt much like smiling. One doesn't when one has received a shock,' she said pointedly.

He regarded her gravely, his eyes glinting as he spoke in a low tone. 'Can we forget it for this evening? Let's see if we can enjoy ourselves just for a change. Is it a promise?'

'Yes, I—I suppose so.' Gazing up at him, Sara wondered if she looked as hypnotised as she felt.

He went on, 'Believe me, I feel sorry for Tom, Dick and Harry, or whoever. If one dares to come near he'll get short shrift. He'll be sent into orbit.'

Another faint smile touched her lips, although she knew that this idle chatter was a mere ploy to coax her into an amenable frame of mind—one that would make her more favourably disposed to whatever suggestion *he* had in mind. However, she said nothing, and within a short time she was again sitting beside him in the car.

The drive to the Wairakei Hotel took only a short time, and once more Sara was assailed by a feeling of unreality. Was it only seven hours since Leon had peered at her through the glass of the salon door? Was it only six hours since she'd felt the full impact of this infuriating situation—only five hours since she'd awakened to the fact that she must learn to cope with its frustration?

And look at her now—dressed in her best and being taken out to dinner by this man who had intruded into her life. Did this mean she was already learning to cope? Nor did it seem possible to believe she had known him for only those few hours. Instead, she felt as if she had known him for years.

And then honesty compelled her to admit that this unexpected complacency had been engendered by the man himself. This man whose hands looked so firm and steady as they rested lightly on the steering wheel—this man whose entire being oozed with vitality, and with a virility that set him apart from every other man she knew, and who seemed to be having an effect on her emotions.

On arrival at the hotel he led her into a lounge where drinks were served, and the fact that he took her arm possessively when guiding her to a secluded corner caused her pleasure rather than any hint of irritation. A few sips of the potent sherry he ordered served only to make her feel even more relaxed, while several more sips loosened her tongue.

'Tell me about the salon,' he prompted as though he had decided that easy conversation was necessary. 'It's a unisex, I presume?'

'Of course. We have numerous male clients.'

'If I come in for a haircut you'll promise not to take a snip at my ear and then claim it was an accident?'

'Well, it is a tempting thought,' Sara agreed. 'A mere touch of the scissors and the lobe bleeds profusely, but I've no wish to see a man rush from the salon with blood streaming down his neck. It's not the way to win clients and encourage business. However, if you're nervous I'll leave you in Pam's hands. She's my first assistant and a very capable hair-stylist.'

'I shall insist on your own ministrations,' Leon assured her.

'I'll take care to avoid your ears,' she promised gravely.

'You'll go for my throat instead?' he queried with deceptive mildness while watching her narrowly.

'Again, it's a tempting thought,' she returned in an equally bland tone. 'We'll just have to wait and see how things turn out.'

'I can see you're still poised and ready to jump into the fray,' he accused with an edge to his voice. 'Obviously there's small hope of a pleasant evening.'

There and then Sara made a vow that the evening would be a pleasant one. And even if he did have a purpose in buttering her up with costly entertainment, it was a game that two could play. She would respond by offering bright company to show her appreciation.

The cottage would not be mentioned, she decided. However, if the subject of demolishing it did happen to arise she would not argue about it. She would merely smile and bide her time, hoping that at some future date she would be able to make him see that such an idea was impossible.

A short time later they were ushered to a table, where they were served a superb meal. The wine Leon ordered made Sara feel slightly light-headed, and she found herself chatting amicably until she realised he was regarding her with a hint of amusement. 'I'm talking too much,' she admitted, pausing abruptly.

'Not at all,' he assured her. 'I'm interested to see the real you, rather than the defensive person who discovered me peering at her through the salon door. I must say I like this one much better. She's rather sweet and she has humour. Further, she's now handling this rather difficult situation with aplomb.'

His words sent a glow through her, yet her face remained serious as she said, 'I'll confess I've been rocked today, but I'm now looking on it as being part of the trauma of losing Jane.'

'In this life one learns to deal with hard knocks. My own lessons came early with the loss of my parents.' Leon paused, regarding her in silence for several moments before he added, 'And incidentally, I don't usually have such confidences dragged from me, especially by a stranger—yet for some unknown reason I've been unable to look on you as a stranger.'

His words gave her a feeling of satisfaction, although she was unable to understand why this should be so, and she was still pondering the question when she received her second severe jolt of the day. It came from the sound of a voice that hauled back her own past.

The tall fair-haired man who had paused at their table was well dressed, and his mocking drawl hit her ears. 'Well, well, well, if it isn't Sara! Long time no see!'

Startled, she almost dropped her dessert spoon as she looked up to find a pair of light grey eyes regarding her with interest, and for several moments she was unable to speak while she continued to stare at him blankly.

The man spoke again, even more mockingly than before. 'Never let it be said that you've forgotten *me*— Sara.'

Leon rose to his feet to lean across the table and query in a barely audible voice, 'Could this be Tom, Dick or Harry?'

Sara found her wits and her tongue. 'No. Actually, it's Terry. Terry Purvis—Leon Longley,' she introduced, then turning to the tall fair man she said sweetly, 'Yes, I'm afraid I had forgotten you—*completely*.'

It was more or less true, even if it had been an effort that had taken time, and now Terry Purvis was the last man she wanted to see, especially at this particular moment. The sight of him almost caused her to choke on the last spoonful of dessert, but outwardly she remained calm, and it was only by grasping at control that she kept a steady hand while pouring coffee for Leon and herself.

CHAPTER FOUR

THE two men favoured each other with little more than a brief nod, then Terry spoke casually to Sara. 'I hear you now have your own salon.'

Her tone was equally casual. 'Your spies have been out and around this way?'

He went on, 'I happened to meet the woman you worked for before you fled to Taupo. We were attending the same function.'

Sara said nothing while waiting to hear more. What on earth had she ever seen in this man? she now wondered with clearer and more mature vision.

'Apparently your mother had been into the salon, and of course you'd been discussed,' Terry went on.

'Really?' Sara's voice remained cool. She knew Leon was listening with avid interest, despite the inscrutable expression on his face.

'I also learnt you'd suffered a recent bereavement,' Terry added.

'Yes. My great-aunt with whom I was living passed away——'

'I trust she did the right thing by you?' he cut in easily.

She ignored the question in his voice. 'Jane was always very kind to me.' Then, changing the subject abruptly, she asked in a sweet tone, 'How is Louise? Is she here with you?'

His sandy brows rose almost into his fair hair. 'Louise? Louise who?'

Sara felt shocked, but managed to say evenly, 'Louise—your wife. The girl you married, of course. Whom else could I possibly mean?'

Terry's face cleared. 'Oh, then you haven't heard?'

'Heard what?' His tone puzzled her.

57

'That affair ended ages ago. Actually, it didn't last for long.'

She felt confused. 'Correct me if I'm wrong, but you *did* marry Louise?'

Terry spoke airily. 'Oh, yes, we married. And we parted. It's all over now. The divorce has gone through, the goods and chattels nicely divided.' A satisfied grin spread over his face.

Leon, who had listened with interest, now spoke quietly. 'You did well out of it, I presume?'

Terry's grin widened. 'You could say so. Her old man's well heeled and we'd been nicely set up in a home with all the trimmings. But the love nest developed thistles and thorns. We just didn't get on. Not like——' He glanced towards Sara, then fell silent.

Sara froze as she realised he had been about to say *not like Sara and I.* And now a glance at Leon's amused expression told her he guessed there had been something between herself and this man. Her cheeks became slightly flushed, but she said nothing.

Further irritation arose as Terry said in a jovial voice, 'I'll see you again some time. I come to Taupo quite often these days—our accountancy firm has an office here. Incidentally, I'm now with a different firm.'

Sara spoke quickly. 'I'm afraid I'm kept very busy.'

He gave a light laugh. 'Busy? Doing what?'

'You're forgetting I run a business, and I have a house and garden to keep in order. There's little time for social life.'

His interest sharpened. 'That's right, the salon woman said you've inherited a house in Taupo——'

Leon cut into his words. 'Where would she get that information?'

Sara's shoulders lifted in a slight shrug. 'From Mother, I suppose. Jane never made any secret of—of those particular intentions.'

Terry said, 'I must come and view the premises.'

Leon snapped a question. 'Didn't you hear the lady say she'd be busy?'

Terry gave a smug grin. 'I can remember the time when the same lady was never too busy to see me.'

Sara said, 'That was four years ago, Terry—before you married Louise.' She took a deep breath, then added with a hint of firm dismissal, 'Will you excuse us while we enjoy our coffee?'

His light grey eyes flashed with amusement. 'Full of confidence these days, are we? By the look of us we're no longer the timid mouse of bygone days.'

She sent him a level glance. 'You can say we've matured. We've gathered a great deal more common sense.' Then she turned away before a surge of bitterness forced her to add, And you can say we're no longer the lovelorn idiot of past years—the one you led along the path of hope, only to shut the door in her face.

'Well, as I said, we'll meet again,' he declared breezily, and left their table to saunter towards the door.

Leon's eyes narrowed as he watched Terry's departure. 'I believe that fellow has hurt you at some time,' he observed in a voice that held firm conviction.

'What makes you so sure about that?' Sara hedged.

'I sensed the atmosphere between you, especially when he suggested you'd "fled" to Taupo. People don't flee without cause.' He paused to look at her searchingly. 'Care to tell me about it?'

She stared into her coffee-cup. 'I don't think so.'

'Then allow me to tell you.' He leaned forward and spoke in a manner that defied contradiction. 'You were twenty at the time, stricken by a severe illness known as being in love.'

'It's common among girls barely out of their teens,' she defended.

'You expected to become engaged to him,' Leon pursued relentlessly. 'Am I right?'

Her eyes clouded as she conceded, 'I suppose that just about sums up the situation.'

'But something happened. I can see by your face that it did.'

'If you don't mind, I've no wish to discuss it.' The memory of that ghastly night returned to hit her with full force.

His face was stern. 'You'd be wise to do so. Bringing matters out into the open helps to put them into perspective. It will enable you to cope when he does turn up, as he most surely will.'

Sara looked at him doubtfully. Was he probing into her past from mere curiosity, or was he being genuinely helpful? Then, almost against her will, she found the confession being dragged from her.

'I've hardly spoken of it since I wept on my grandmother's shoulder. Mother was inclined to brush it aside as being a mere incident. She seemed to consider it had happened for the best.'

'Mothers are often right,' Leon commented.

'Gran realised I'd been really shocked. She arranged for me to stay with her sister Jane for a while, and then the salon job came up. I mean the one here in Taupo.' Why was she opening up to him in this manner? she wondered.

'What actually brought on all this trauma?' Leon asked softly.

She hesitated, then decided that as she'd told him so much she might as well tell him the rest. Self-consciously she said, 'Looking back, I can see that I'd been utterly stupid. Everyone knew how I felt about Terry because I was too naïve to hide it. It probably shone out of my face. And then Louise's twenty-first birthday party was held. It was quite a large affair.'

'Louise being one of your friends?' he guessed.

'Yes. And she was also the daughter of Terry's boss.'

'For whom he no longer works, you'll notice.'

'I'm not surprised.' She fell silent, as though reluctant to relive those moments of pain, but eventually she drew a deep breath and said, 'Well, at the height of the party

Terry and Louise's engagement was announced. And while everyone raised their glasses, they all turned to look at me. I'll never forget it—I thought I'd die of shame.'

'But you didn't. So what did you do instead?'

'I kissed Louise in an effort to show everyone I didn't care and that I was happy for her, then I slipped from the room and ran along the street.'

'With tears streaming down your cheeks?'

She nodded. 'Somebody—one of the men—caught up with me. He put me in his car and drove me home.'

'So while the bells pealed for Louise, they tolled for you.'

'I suppose so,' she shrugged. 'Next day Terry came to see me. He tried to explain that I'd taken too much for granted, and obviously he was right.'

'And since then the bells have tolled for Louise. Personally, I consider you had a lucky escape,' said Leon.

She stared unseeingly into her coffee-cup. 'Perhaps. Who can tell about these things?' she queried with a sigh.

His eyes became penetrating while he frowned at her sternly. 'Don't tell me you still have feelings left for this fellow who deserted you for the boss's daughter?'

Her smile held pathos. 'It took me a long time to get over it.'

'I'm wondering if you are over it, despite the years.'

Sara nodded vigorously, but said nothing.

His eyes narrowed as they surveyed her. 'I don't believe you,' he declared in a hard tone. 'You're merely trying to convince yourself.'

She continued to look at him in silence. For some reason she was unable to define she did not deny the accusation, and while she knew that Leon was mistaken in assuming she still retained feelings of affection for Terry, she told herself it was not his concern. Nor did his intrusion into her home give him the right to put her emotions under the microscope.

Again she pleaded, 'If you don't mind, I'd rather not discuss it.'

But he refused to be finished with the subject, and, watching her from across the table, he persisted, 'I can almost imagine your reaction to the affair. You lost faith in the male of the species. You refused to go out with other men.'

Surprised by his perception, she admitted, 'Actually, I turned into something of a hermit. Jane became thoroughly impatient with me, although she tried to understand.'

'She suspected you were still hankering after Purvis?'

'She declared I was wasting my time by clinging to a bad dream, but to be honest I felt distrustful of all men. I—I couldn't tolerate the thought of becoming involved again.'

'I presume you mean with someone other than Purvis. They say love never dies, but I can hardly believe you'd be foolish enough to keep pining for a man who had already let you down to further his own career.' Leon paused to regard her thoughtfully, then added, 'Jane was right when she told John Abernethy you needed somebody to guide you along the right track.'

Her head jerked up. 'Jane said that? I don't believe it!'

He shrugged. 'I can only repeat what the old boy let slip.'

Sara's eyes widened as indignation began to simmer. 'Is that why she left half the property to you? Are you supposed to guide me towards what's best to be done with it?'

'I suspect he thought that that was what she had in mind, to say nothing of your need for someone to take care of you.'

'In that case he's got his wires crossed,' she declared with conviction. 'Not for one moment do I believe Jane said that. She knew I've been able to take care of myself for—for *years*.'

'Then see that you continue to do so when His Nibs turns up.'

'You mean Terry? What makes you so sure he'll give me as much as a second thought?'

'Good grief, it's elementary!' exclaimed Leon. 'He thinks you now own a property at Taupo. Don't you realise that real estate at Taupo is valuable?'

'I—I haven't given it much thought,' she admitted.

'Then it's high time you did, because he'll be back like the proverbial homing pigeon.'

'He'll get no billing and cooing from me,' she retorted crossly.

His voice held a sardonic note. 'That's something I'm inclined to doubt, especially as you didn't tell him you own only half the property. Holding it out as bait, were you?'

'Certainly not!' she snapped.

'Then why the omission?'

'Because it's not his concern, and in any case I—I'm still finding difficulty in believing it myself.'

'You will after you've been to see John Abernethy,' Leon assured her. 'And after that the dual ownership should be enough to dampen the Purvis ardour—especially when he finds what he'll consider to be a cuckoo in the nest,' he added with a chuckle.

His words caused her to exclaim in horrified tones, 'He'll tell everyone you're living in my house and that—that——'

'We're shacked up together in sin?' he queried silkily, while an even deeper chuckle shook his frame.

Sara became angry. 'It's all very well for you to think it's funny, but it's no laughing matter. He'll tell the world,' she hissed in a low voice. 'My parents and grandmother will be *furious*! They're very straitlaced, they don't hold with loose living.'

'Then they'll just have to blame Jane,' he commented drily. 'They'll have to be told that Jane threw us into the same bed——'

'*She did not!*' Sara snapped.

He yawned. 'I'm becoming bored with these silly hysterics. Have you forgotten I promised to find someone to live with us?'

'But you haven't even told me her name,' she protested.

'It's Edith Sellwood. She's a divorcee who went to school with my mother. I understand they used to sit together, and when my parents were married she was Mother's bridesmaid.'

'Well, I hope she'll come to us soon.'

'I'll phone her tomorrow,' he promised.

'What makes you so sure she'll come?' asked Sara.

'The fact that she loves Lake Taupo—plus the fact that she's a spender who can always do with extra cash.'

'And because you've asked her?' Sara put in with sudden perception.

'It's—possible.' His eyes were hooded.

Instinct niggled at her, causing her to say, 'In that case she must have a special interest in you.'

'Didn't I tell you she's an old friend?'

'Even so, it'll probably cost a lot,' she said apprehensively.

'That doesn't matter if it puts your parents' minds at rest.'

She felt guilty that her own attitude should be proving expensive for him, but reminded herself that if he insisted on moving into the cottage it was up to him to see that she was not being compromised. Granted, this was a day and age when the modern view made it more acceptable for young people to live together, but that was no reason for her to drop her own old-fashioned standards. Nor did she see why his decision should be allowed to upset her parents.

'Something continues to concern you,' he observed, watching the expressions flitting across her face.

She hesitated, then asked, 'Can you afford what this will probably cost? In fairness, I should pay half.'

He laughed. 'Thank you for offering, but I wouldn't tolerate such a situation. I can assure you it won't run me into debt.'

He's generous, she conceded within her mind, then shied away from the subject of money by saying, 'Perhaps you could tell me more about Mrs Sellwood.'

'Edith? I suppose she's rising towards sixty. Since the divorce she's earned extra money by caring for elderly people or children while other members of a household are away on holiday. I'm hoping she's unoccupied at this present time.'

'And if she isn't?'

'We'll have to find somebody else, and that might take time. In the meantime we'll keep our fingers crossed for luck with Edith, because she's a very capable person who'll remove the worry of all household chores from your shoulders.'

Sara gave a rueful smile. 'I'll admit the windows don't clean themselves while I'm at the salon, nor does the vacuum pop out of the cupboard and run over the carpets.'

Darkness had fallen by the time they left the hotel. The sky was clear, and as they walked to where the car was parked the brilliance of the heavens drew their gaze towards the countless millions of sparkling pinpoints.

Leon paused, one hand on her arm drawing her closer to him, while the other pointed skyward. 'There's the Southern Cross, seen only in the southern hemisphere. Have you ever seen the four main pointers shine so brightly?' he asked casually.

She shook her head while gazing upward, the stars changing to a white blur as she became conscious of his nearness. His hand on her arm made her pulses leap, while the aura of his masculinity washed over her, causing sensations as unexpected as they were rare. Also unexpected was the kiss he dropped on her upturned brow.

Startled, she sprang away from him. 'You've got a nerve!' she gasped, aware that her heart had given a lurch.

He grinned at her through the gloom. 'Unpleasant, was it?'

'No, but——' Her blood was still racing through her veins.

His stare became intense. 'Allergic to being kissed, are you?'

A grip on her control enabled her to say in firm tones, 'I'm not in the habit of allowing strangers to take liberties.'

'You disappoint me. I felt sure I'd progressed beyond the state of being a stranger.' Leon remained silent until they reached the car, where he went on in a sardonic tone, 'Perhaps it's just that you're cold. Possibly it's the reason why Purvis stopped kissing you and began kissing Louise.' He paused again, looking at her intently. 'No, I don't really believe you're completely frigid.'

Sara considered the remark while taking her seat in the car, then, feeling that an answer was expected of her, she parried, 'Why should you be interested in whether or not I'm cold?'

'Because the thought of living with an iceberg makes me feel chilly. I like a warm person. Now take Megan, for instance—she's a hot dish,' Leon added casually as the car turned on to the highway and headed towards Taupo.

She turned to stare at his profile. 'Megan? Who's Megan?'

'She's Edith Sellwood's daughter. Didn't I mention her?'

'You know very well you didn't mention her! But that's not surprising, because I've had to drag every scrap of information about Mrs Sellwood from you.'

'Being garrulous about other people is not part of my nature,' he said in a tone that was almost a reprimand. 'However, I'll try to fill in a few details. I've been told that in her younger days Edith was what's known as a beautiful redhead. Now she's considered to be a handsome woman. She married an accountant, but the marriage didn't last. Megan, their only child, has never lost touch with her father, and she now works a computer in his office.'

'Megan is also a—a beautiful redhead?' The question came casually, although Sara wasn't sure why she should be interested.

'I suppose you could say so. I'm told she's the image of the way her mother looked at that age.'

'At what age? How old is she?' The queries slipped out.

'A little younger than I am.' Leon sent her a rapid glance. 'Why the questionnaire—and such interest in Megan?'

Sara remained silent while pondering that same question. Indeed, why was she interested in Megan Sellwood? Yet instinct seemed to push questions concerning the girl about in her mind. 'I suppose Megan is married, or at least engaged?' she asked at last, the words being forced from her by something she was unable to define.

Leon laughed. 'If she is she's kept it a dark secret from me.'

'Does that mean you'd know of any involvement she might have? Are you so close to each other?' She held her breath, awaiting the answer, and again she queried her own interest.

He ignored the latter question as he said, 'Lengthy family association, I suppose—and because she usually lets me know what's going on in her life.'

'How nice for her to have a willing listener—and for you to have such a close friend, someone who's so *warm*!'

The dashboard lights betrayed his frown. 'Something about Megan worries you before you've even met her?'

Sara ignored the question by asking one of her own. 'Who says I'll meet her?'

'If Edith is with us, Megan is sure to visit her mother, at least during the weekend.'

She said nothing, while trying to assure herself that a visit from Megan Sellwood would not prove to be a problem. If it did she'd face it when it arose.

They reached home with little more being said. The car was driven into the cleared space in the double garage, then the roller doors were closed. In the kitchen Sara felt a sense of anticlimax which made her pause to ask, 'Would you like more coffee?'

Leon turned to face her. 'No, thank you—but I'd like to clear my mind on one certain point. It's the question of temperature.'

She was puzzled. 'Temperature? I don't understand.'

'I accused you of being cold. Now's your big opportunity to prove you're not.' Two steps closed the gap between them, his hands gripping her arms as he drew her against him. For several brief moments he stared down into her face while she gazed up at him wordlessly.

Fighting the surge of excitement building within her body, she gasped. 'Why is it necessary for me to prove anything?'

'You can look on it as a tactical manoeuvre in the battle between us. Demolition—or maintenance?'

She gaped at him incredulously. 'Are you hinting that a few kisses from me will save the cottage from being demolished?'

'Who says I'll be satisfied with a few?' he murmured, then lowered his head to find her lips in a kiss that was gentle yet seductive until it deepened to betray the passion lurking beneath the surface. And with its intensity his arms held her even closer so that she became vitally aware of his arousal.

A wave of indignation swept through her, while she told herself he had a colossal nerve to take this liberty on such short acquaintance. Her hands went to his chest with the intention of pushing him away, but suddenly a force stronger than herself killed her protest. The pressure in her arms weakened, while her anger switched to something that resembled clearer thinking.

To demolish or maintain, he had said. Was it possible that a few kisses from her *could* save the cottage? She would have to be naïve to believe so—or to trust his word to this extent. Still, anything was worth trying if it enabled her to keep her promise to Jane.

And this decision had nothing to do with the fact that his lips were now nuzzling gently at her own, and that she was still in his arms. After all, her aim must be towards mutual agreement, and that meant closer relations with this—this intruder.

But even as she assured herself that these were her reasons for tolerating his embrace, she became aware that his arms had dropped to his sides and that he had stepped away from her. She also noticed that his face held a guarded expression, almost as though he already regretted those moments of closeness and feared she might take too much meaning from them.

His next words seemed to prove this when he informed her in a blunt tone, 'There's no need for you to lock your bedroom door.'

'No? Well, that's a relief. Nevertheless I shall do so, despite your assurance.' She left him abruptly, her heart still pounding more rapidly than she would have thought possible.

Later, as she prepared for bed, she endeavoured to forget the incident. It meant nothing, she assured herself. But instead of closing her eyes as quickly as usual she twisted and turned while the events of the day flooded her mind to stir a turmoil that kept sleep at bay. And the closer she examined each event in turn, the more wakeful and disturbed she became.

Sleep claimed her at last, but next morning she felt heavy-eyed—a fact which did not escape Leon's notice when she walked into the kitchen.

'You slept badly?' he queried in a polite tone.

'Like a log,' she lied with a touch of defiance. 'What could make you imagine otherwise?'

'Those shadows round your eyes. There was no need for you to lie awake fearing I'd break down your door or climb in the window. I thought I'd assured you I had no interest——'

'No interest in me personally,' she interrupted angrily. 'Your only interest lies in the property.'

'I've no interest in a girl who continually tries my patience,' he rasped. 'Why can't you be grateful for the extra protection afforded by having a man in the house?'

'Grateful? Huh! I don't need a man in the house,' she stormed. 'Men are untrustworthy creatures who toss a girl aside as easily as they dropped their childhood toys. I've already learnt——' She stopped abruptly, biting her lip.

'That particular lesson?' he concluded softly for her.

Sara remained silent, appalled by her own outburst.

He considered her thoughtfully. 'What can I say to drag you out of this fretful mood? Unless you snap out of it our picnic will be ruined, and you wouldn't like that,' he mocked.

'Picnic!' she echoed scornfully. 'Never have I felt less like going on a picnic!'

'But you will be—er—gracious enough to come?'

'I suppose so,' she conceded with reluctance. 'I'll make sandwiches—but before we leave I'll spend a short time in the garden.'

'You mean actually gardening?'

'What else?' It felt good to show determination on her own account, just in case he had decided on the exact moment of their departure. Nor had perversity anything to do with her sudden decision, she assured herself.

Leon frowned. 'You have a large job in mind?'

'No.' Already she was capitulating. 'It's just that some of the self-seeded borage plants must be transplanted before they grow too large. It's the herb with flowers like sky-blue stars.'

'In what way would Jane use borage?' he queried.

'In drinks. She maintained that borage cheered the heart.'

Amused, he said, 'That's strange—I thought the cup that cheered was made from something entirely different. May I suggest you try nibbling a few leaves while you're out there?'

The hint to shake herself into a more pleasant frame of mind gave him the last word, she realised resentfully. Nor had he offered the slightest atom of comfort to remove the bleakness which he knew held her in a firm grip. Couldn't he understand that Jane's wishes, recorded by a few strokes of a pen, had altered her life? And now she must face up to the situation while becoming accustomed to this changed state of affairs.

The thoughts continued to rile her as she knelt on the path to lift and separate the small borage plants. Leon had made no further attempt to kiss her, she also realised, and this seemed to prove that last night's embrace had been nothing more than a casual gesture. It also implied that she was something to be picked up or put down according to his whim.

Crossly, she scrambled to her feet, the plant in her hand losing soil, and as she turned to move away she became aware of Iris Radcliffe's pale blue eyes watching her from across the dividing fence.

'Good morning, dear,' the neighbour called. 'Did you have a happy evening last night? I saw you go out, although you weren't very late in coming home. It's all part of Neighbourhood Watch,' she explained in the virtuous voice Sara had heard before.

'We went out to dinner,' she felt obliged to explain without quite knowing why she should do so.

'How nice for you, dear,' Iris cooed. 'You've had so much to contend with recently—and I guessed you must have been feeling weary, because the house was in

darkness within such a short time,' she added inno-
cently, watching Sara through narrowed lids.

Sara swallowed, then said faintly, 'Was it? I—I really
had no idea of the time——'

'Oh well, one doesn't bother about *time* when one has
such *handsome* company.' Iris sent a knowing smile
across the fence. 'Is he very romantic to be with?' she
queried coyly.

'I don't know what you mean, Mrs Radcliffe.' Sara
tossed the words at her haughtily.

'I think you do, my dear—and I'm sure Jane would
be worried.'

'Would she indeed? Mrs Radcliffe, you've just come
up with the joke of the century!' But there was no smile
on Sara's face as she dropped the plant and strode into
the kitchen.

Leon was there, leaning over his land use map which
he had spread on the table. He glanced up as she came
in, his eyes narrowing as he studied her face. 'What's
happened? You look really upset—even more so than
when you went out to become cheerful with borage.'

'Have you phoned Edith Sellwood yet?' she
demanded.

His brows rose. 'What's brought on this extra
aggression?'

'That woman next door—she's watching our every
move, even to when the lights go out!'

He grinned. 'You could invite her in to observe what
goes on in the dark—but warn her that it can't be billed
as prime entertainment.'

Sara said agitatedly, 'Can't you understand the way
her mind is working? She'll tell the world the worst is
happening.'

'You mean she's got us in bed together?'

'*Yes*, if you must know.' She swung round and strode
into the laundry, where she began to wash the earth from
her hands.

He followed her to the door. 'I must say it's a lovely thought.'

'Please be serious,' she flung over her shoulder, while an upsurge of frustration almost caused her to stamp a foot in rage.

'You don't think it's a lovely thought?' he drawled.

She turned crimson. 'Of course not! It's a—a *ghastly* thought——' The words died on her lips as honesty forced her to wonder if the thought of being in bed with this man was really so ghastly after all.

'You're saying you've never known the joy of lying naked beside a man in bed?' he persisted softly.

'Mind your own blasted business!' she almost shouted. 'And please stop being ridiculous. Just tell me—*have you phoned Edith Sellwood*?'

'Yes. I spoke to her while you were lapping up brightness from the borage seedlings.'

Sara ignored his levity. Wiping her hands, she stared at him across the towel, her hazel eyes wide with anxiety. 'What did she say?'

'She promised to see what she could do.'

'Is that all?' Her words echoed dismay.

'Did you expect her to drop everything and rush here at once?' he asked.

'Did you explain the seriousness of the situation?' Sara demanded.

'Very clearly. She said she'd let us know.'

'Did she, indeed? And when will that be?' She brushed past him impatiently to return to the kitchen, then turned to regard him with a look steeped in deep suspicion. 'To be honest, I can't help wondering if you really did phone her.'

He scowled as he rasped, 'Are you calling me a liar?'

'Men are good at lying,' she snapped back at him, pacing about the room in a new frenzy of impatience.

'Can't you simmer down?' he snarled. 'You're building this into something that's out of all proportion.'

'You may think so, but I don't,' she informed him loftily. However, his words had the effect of causing her to become calmer, and as she began to think more clearly she came to a decision. Her voice ringing with determination, she said, 'I'm afraid I can't wait for Mrs Sellwood to make up her mind. First thing tomorrow morning I'll go to the employment agency to see if they can come up with a suitable person.'

'You'll really do that?' Leon's mouth was tight.

'Yes. It'll be much quicker. I might even come home with someone at lunchtime,' she said hopefully.

'It pleases you to ignore the fact that I've already spoken to Edith?' he snapped coldly.

'You can tell her not to bother,' she retorted airily. 'I was stupid not to have thought of the employment agency to begin with.'

His anger turned to amusement. 'Aren't you forgetting?' he drawled lazily.

'Forgetting?' Sara looked at him sharply, the suspicion that he was laughing at her growing steadily.

'The matter of old Abernethy. Didn't you intend rushing to him first thing in the morning, feet barely touching the ground?'

'I have not forgotten Mr Abernethy,' she told him with an edge to her voice. 'I'll go to him first and then to the agency.'

'Abernethy, and the task of getting me out of the house, taking top priority,' he jeered.

'You could say so,' she told him with utter frankness. 'Can't you see that—that without you in the house there'll be no need for this other person?'

Leon stepped closer to glare down into her face. 'You're finding my presence so very obnoxious?'

'I didn't say that.' She looked away from him, realising that his presence was anything but obnoxious. In fact there were odd moments when she quite liked it, but this thought was so confusing she pushed it away from her mind. What was the matter with her? Why couldn't she think clearly?

Staring up at him, she became aware that her breath had quickened and that his closeness disturbed her, so she turned and moved away to gaze unseeingly through the window. And it was there that she found herself startled by the knowledge that at heart she didn't want Leon to leave. Only, of course, because his presence would keep Terry Purvis away from her. Yes, that was the only reason.

CHAPTER FIVE

LEON regarded Sara with amused tolerance. 'I'll be interested to learn Abernethy's reaction to your request for my eviction.'

'You're not the only subject I want to discuss with him,' she admitted. 'I'm hoping he'll be able to tell me what brought my great-aunt to her decision. Despite her promises to me she changed her mind—and I need to know why.'

'Women are experts at changing their minds.'

His cynical remark went over her head while she continued with a slight tremor in her voice, 'I can't help wondering if she was upset with me for some reason— yet not once did we have cross words or a quarrel of any sort. Mr Abernethy might be able to give me a reason for her change of mind.'

'It's possible—but highly improbable,' he shrugged.

'You mean he'd be unlikely to tell me, even if he knew?'

'Haven't you heard of client confidentiality? He'll merely point out that Jane Patterson left a record of her wishes, and that's all there is to it.'

Sara sighed inwardly, fearing Leon could be right, and she also realised that this discussion was having a depressing effect on her, so she changed the subject by saying, 'I'll fetch the picnic basket from the laundry.'

Within a short time she had filled the small hamper with items of food taken from the fridge, or snatched from the deep freeze and thawed in the microwave.

Leon watched with interest. 'You appear to have picnic fare on hand,' he remarked.

'Jane enjoyed being taken for a drive and then stopping for lunch beside the lake,' she explained briefly.

'I can believe you really were good to her.' Then, moving closer to examine the contents of the basket hamper, he placed a hand on her shoulder. 'Who are the other four fellows?'

'What?' she queried.

'You've packed enough for at least six people.' Pressure came from his fingers as he added, 'There's an old saying about the way to a man's heart being through his stomach.'

Sara was aghast that he should have such a thought. It caused her to draw a sharp breath as she shrugged his hand from her shoulder and snapped, 'One more remark like that and I'll refuse to go with you! In the meantime, I'll remove these date cookies as punishment——'

'Like hell you will!' A quick movement of his hand grabbed her arm and spun her round to face him, then, scowling down at her, he gritted, 'I was only joking. I'm well aware that beneath any pleasant exterior you see fit to present, you positively hate my guts.'

She returned his gaze unflinchingly. 'You're entirely wrong. I have no hatred for you whatever.'

'Despite the fact that I've swept half your inheritance from your grasp? I'm afraid it will take more than a little effort to convince me on that score.' He continued to stare searchingly into her face as he added, 'I'll admit it came to me as a pleasant surprise—although I can understand that to you it must be a bitter blow.'

She turned away, unwilling to let him read the truth of his words in her eyes. 'You couldn't possibly understand how I've felt. I've tried to brainwash myself into accepting that if this was Jane's wish—well, so be it.'

His eyes seemed to bore into her. 'Yet you'll be on old Abernethy's doorstep at daybreak—or almost.'

'I told you, I need to know *why*.'

He laughed, then jeered softly, 'You're not fooling me, Sara.'

His tone surprised her. 'What do you mean?' she queried.

'You know perfectly well that no will is final until probate has been granted by the Supreme Court, and that usually takes time. In the meantime you intend asking Abernethy to get me out of the house until probate has been granted.'

Her eyes widened with sudden interest. 'I'd forgotten about probate—but now you've pointed the way to a good idea.'

A shade of annoyance crossed his face as he said, 'I'll be most interested to learn the result of your chat with Abernethy.'

'That's if I choose to tell you,' she flashed at him.

'You will, even if I have to shake it out of you. Now then, are we ready to leave?'

'As soon as I've changed,' she retorted abruptly.

'I like you as you are in those green shorts. Your bare legs are very shapely.'

Sara ignored the compliment by hastening to her bedroom, where she changed into a lilac leisure suit, ran a comb through her blonde hair and attended to her make-up. As she did so she struggled with mixed feelings that caused questions to jump about in her mind.

What was the matter with her? One moment she was delighted to be going out with Leon, while the next instant found her grasping at a plan to be rid of him. Was he also planning to be rid of her? The thought was disturbing, and again the most vital question of all plagued her mind. Why had she been placed in this situation?

When she went outdoors she saw that the hamper had been put into the Daimler which now stood waiting in the drive. The garage doors had been closed, and as she locked the back door her eyes went to the kitchen window of the house next door. A slight movement of shadow behind the curtains told her that Neighbourhood Watch was in operation, even in mid-morning, but she made no further comment regarding Iris Radcliffe's avid interest in their movements.

The drive along the lakefront was completed in silence, but eventually Sara was forced to send a rapid glance towards the handsome profile beside her. There were grim lines about the mouth, she noticed, deciding it was a sure sign of Leon's suppressed anger.

'I appear to have said something that's really annoyed you,' she said in a quiet voice.

His tone was casual as he shrugged the suggestion away. 'My emotions are never upset by trivial remarks.'

'Trivial! Huh!' She controlled her temper while they crossed the bridge where the Waikato River tumbled from the lake. Minutes later they passed the turn-off to the Huka Falls, but when Leon took a right-hand turn a short distance downriver from the falls she became alert. Glancing at him, she said, 'This road leads to the Aratiatia Rapids. It doesn't lead to land for development—which I'm sure is all you're interested in seeing.'

'I know exactly where it leads,' he retorted testily. 'It's just that I haven't seen the rapids for years, and as we're so near them——'

She sighed. 'We're fortunate they still exist. You probably know that when the Aratiatia power station was built the plan was to do away with the rapids, but as they're one of the awe-inspiring sights of the district there was a public outcry at the thought of them being destroyed.'

Leon glanced at his watch. 'I understand the Electricity Department came up with a compromise which allows huge floodgates in the dam to be opened twice daily. The siren should be sounding quite soon.'

They parked the car, then walked along the track towards one of the viewpoints. Nor were they the only people who had come to see the rapids, and Sara felt a sinking feeling when she saw Terry Purvis standing a short distance away. He appeared to be with a group of friends, and she hoped he would not notice her.

The viewpoint Leon had led her to showed the narrow rocky ravine to advantage, and they were able to gaze along its stark walls which rose above a floor dampened by a few barely connected pools and runlets. Then, as the sound of the siren came to their ears, each vantage point became filled with people wanting to observe the overpowering spectacle that was about to fill the tight-walled passage below them.

Within five minutes the torrent was there, gushing along the twisted ravine in a frenzied flood that crashed and pounded at the walls. It foamed into a seething mass of jets and spurts, and as the sound of its roar rose on the air the ground seemed to tremble.

'It frightens me,' Sara admitted above the noise. She knew that the close proximity of others in the viewpoint had caused Leon to stand behind her, yet despite their presence his arms went round her waist and she felt her back being pressed against him.

'Do you feel hypnotised into jumping in?' he asked in her ear, his lips brushing her cheek.

Startled, she caught her breath, her hands gripping his arms in an effort to remove them, but they remained firmly in place. And then Terry's voice came to her ears, the sound of it causing her to cease the struggle.

The fair-haired man had pushed his way to a position beside them. 'Hi there,' he said above the noise coming from below. 'It's quite a torrent, don't you think? They shut the gates at eleven-thirty and it all disappears until this afternoon, when it's let loose again.'

'Indeed, quite spectacular,' Leon agreed in a dry tone.

Terry looked at Sara. 'I've decided to visit you this afternoon,' he told her.

Leon answered for her, his tone clipped. 'She won't be home.'

'Then this evening?' Terry persisted, his sandy brows raised.

'She'll be busy,' Leon snapped.

'Is she unable to answer for herself?' demanded Terry, making no effort to conceal his irritation, then, as he observed Leon's encircling arms, his tone changed to one of amusement. 'Are you afraid she'll leap away from you?'

'If she does it won't be in your direction,' Leon drawled.

Sara decided it was time to interrupt their discussion. She had no desire for further association with Terry Purvis, so any intentions he had concerning herself must be nipped in the bud, and she felt she'd be wise to make the situation clear here and now.

Speaking rapidly, she said, 'Please understand I have no wish for you to visit me, Terry. As Leon says, I'll be busy.'

Terry's eyes narrowed as they returned to Leon's arms, which were still encircling her waist. 'Busy? Doing what?' he sneered.

The implication behind his words made her flush. 'I'll be minding my own business, and I'll thank you to do the same!' she snapped furiously. Then, turning to Leon, she demanded, 'Have you seen enough of the rapids? May we go?'

'At once,' he agreed.

They pushed their way between people, and as they hastened back to the car Sara felt a sudden satisfaction in the fact that Terry had witnessed Leon's arms about her waist. It might help to keep him at bay. At least, it would act as a deterrent to most men who were less sensitive than Terry Purvis, but with *him* one could never be sure.

However, the day was not to be ruined by petty irritations, Sara decided as she took her seat in the car. First there had been Iris Radcliffe's insinuations about the house being in darkness at an early hour—and now the thoughts and memories of the Terry Purvis affair rose to plague her. She would wipe them from her mind, she told herself firmly. They were all in the past and not to be revived simply because he had appeared in the flesh.

But this did not prove to be easy, because Terry was still hovering in Leon's mind, and as the car turned on to the main highway he sent her a quizzical glance while he questioned casually, 'Did that meeting with Purvis disturb you?'

'Not at all,' she lied, giving a small shrug to show just how nonchalant she felt.

'You've no wish to go home and weep?'

'Weep? Over *him*? You must be joking,' she snapped coldly.

'Good. Just so long as I know you're not stupid enough to do so,' drawled Leon in a voice that held suspicion.

'Could the possibility be any of your business?' she queried with suppressed anger.

'None at all—apart from the fact that I don't suffer fools gladly,' he rasped in a tone that revealed his own irritation.

'You don't have to suffer me at all,' Sara pointed out reasonably. 'You have only to go home to Auckland, from which distance I'd be completely out of sight.'

'Which is something I've no intention of doing,' he assured her crisply, his jaw tightening.

His tone caused her to flick a glance at him, and as she observed the hard line of his mouth enlightenment dawned. For some strange reason the encounter with Terry seemed to have annoyed Leon as much as it had irritated herself.

He had known that Terry was watching them, she decided—and *that* was why he had put his arms about her waist. The action had held no genuine desire to touch her. Instead it had merely been a subtle act of defiance directed at the other man. But for Pete's sake, why had he troubled to do it?

She was still pondering the question when they reached the signpost pointing to Kinloch, a lakeside settlement fourteen miles from Taupo. Leon reduced speed, then turned right to follow the road that wound through undulating country until he stopped at an area reserved for development.

'A place for a retirement village, do you think?' he queried.

'Definitely not!' Sara's negative response held scorn.

He turned to scowl at her. 'Are you being deliberately antagonistic to my *simple* suggestion, or do you really see it as being thoroughly unsuitable?'

'The latter, of course. Elderly people like to be near the lake where they can watch the boats. And they like to take short walks to the shops. This area would deny them such *simple* pleasures.'

His frown deepened. 'Must you throw my emphasis back in my face? Is it because Purvis still niggles at your mind?'

'No, it is not!' she almost shouted at him. 'Can't you understand that the entire subject of property development irks me?'

'Of course. How thoughtless of me,' he mocked. 'Nevertheless you're right about this particular area having definite drawbacks. I can see the firm will have to consult you on all future purchases.'

She ignored his sarcasm. 'The firm? But I thought——'

'That I was on my own? To be precise, I'm the chairman of the company my grandfather formed before he died. Naturally, I can see the disadvantages of the area, but I'm glad they're also apparent to you. It means you can think. You're not just a face.'

'A—a face?' Puzzled, Sara stared straight ahead.

'I like your face with its nice little retroussé nose,' Leon admitted quietly. 'I like the gold sparks that flash in your eyes—and last night I discovered that mouth to be— most kissable.'

She glowed inwardly, but said nothing, and by the time they reached Kinloch something bordering on friendship seemed to have sprung up between them. It was almost as though their discussion had given them a mutual interest, and, sensing its fragile state, Sara realised it must be treated like a delicate flower.

She also made the unexpected discovery that she was no longer interested in bickering with Leon, although what made her so sure about this she was unable to define. Nor did she care to delve into the reasons why an amicable relationship with him should make her feel so much happier.

When they reached Kinloch Leon drove along the waterfront, where a line of tall Lombardy poplars gave shelter to cars parked on the grass, then turned along streets where holiday homes nestled in gardens consisting of trees and shrubs which needed little care.

However, it was the boat marina built in the midst of the housing area that caught Leon's interest, and having examined the moorings and outlet facilities of the extensive man-made harbour he turned to stare at a hill which rose beyond the marina and its neighbouring streets and houses.

Indicating it, he said, 'I think there's a water reservoir on that high mound. There's probably a track leading up to it. Care for a climb?'

Sara nodded. 'It should give us a good view,' she agreed, then surprised herself by admitting silently that she would like to do anything he wanted to do—well, almost!

A short time later they were making their way up a steep grade between hillside scrub, and when Leon held out a helping hand Sara grasped it without hesitation. The firm grip made her nerves tingle, and suddenly the path seemed to be less arduous.

'You're out of breath,' he observed as they reached the top. 'You may lean against me to regain your puff.' The invitation was offered with a grin.

'There's no need, I'm quite all right,' she gasped.

Despite her assurance he drew her against his side, his arm encircling her shoulder. 'There now, relax.'

Nor was she able to do otherwise while becoming conscious of the feeling of comfort that stole over her. It was like an overpowering contentment that forced her to rest her head against his shoulder.

'Isn't that better?' he murmured above her head, the pressure of his arm tightening.

She nodded without speaking, glad to find they were alone on the hilltop.

After that no words were spoken as, standing close together, they looked over to where two headlands stretched to shelter the bay, which was dotted by a variety of sailing craft.

Leon pointed out a launch making its way towards the marina. 'It's probably laden with trout,' he remarked.

His words broke the spell of their closeness, causing Sara to give a shaky laugh as she said, 'Let's sit down.' Then, as they relaxed on the area of soft turf, the words of a client came to her mind, causing her to laugh again.

Leon sent her a quizzical glance. 'What's amusing you?'

'Something said to me by an American lady,' she chuckled. 'She told me that she and her husband had travelled thousands of miles to fish at Taupo, and that he'd spent thousands of dollars on fares and the most expensive equipment—but after he'd taken a few whopping great trout from the lake he'd declared it to be worth every cent.'

'Mighty expensive fish—but I can guess at his feelings.'

She was surprised. 'You can? You haven't admitted to being a dedicated fisherman.'

'I'm not—yet. But who knows? If I'm around for long enough I might become bitten by the bug.'

She digested his words thoughtfully until she said, '*If* you're around? I had the impression that you'd moved in. Is your intention to be around now doubtful?' She held her breath, awaiting his reply.

'It depends on the way things turn out,' he admitted.

'What's that supposed to mean?' she asked lightly, making an effort to sound only half interested.

'Few of us know what surprises lurk round the corner—as you yourself should have realised by now,' Leon added.

'You mean—like the unexpected turning up?'

'That's right.'

'You sound like a prophet of doom. Personally I consider your residence in Rosemary Cottage will depend on whether or not I'll agree to your plans.'

He frowned. 'Have I revealed any definite plans, apart from suggesting that the land could be put to more profitable use?'

Sara lay back on the grass, her hands forming a support for her head, her eyes watching the movement of clouds against the blue sky. 'Perhaps you need time to think about it.' Yes, that was it, she decided. He was a businessman and unlikely to rush into a plan without giving it sufficient thought. And of course he had herself to contend with.

Silence fell between them until his deep voice murmured in her ear, 'You've gone very quiet. What's going on in your head?'

'Nothing in particular,' she lied, startled to notice that he had shifted to a closer position and was now leaning over her. Her pulses leapt with the knowledge that she was about to be kissed, and although her recent thoughts returned to rear their heads she scarcely heard their warning whispers about this being part of his plan to cajole her into his way of thinking.

Staring down at her, his brown eyes held her own in a hypnotic gaze until he lowered his head to brush his lips across her brow, and over her lids, which fluttered closed. Her cheeks were given the same gentle treatment on their flushed surface.

Even as his lips descended to rest softly on her own, nibbling them into response, the warnings persisted, with louder mutterings about this being only part of a softening-up process, and that soon she'd be agreeing to whatever he had in mind.

And while she told herself that this was a game that two could play, she knew it to be only an excuse for her inability to push him away, and for the weakness that forced her to turn her body towards him, betraying her hunger for something more definite.

His arms went round her, holding her in a closer embrace, and as the kiss deepened she became wrapped in a sensual pleasure that sent tingles racing through her nerves. A sigh of contentment escaped her as she responded, and when she felt his arms tighten their clasp, her own crept up to encircle his neck.

At last the kiss ended and he raised his face to look down at her with a hint of mockery. 'I'm amazed you're still here. I thought you'd have sprung to your feet to run screaming down the hill.'

She looked at him wonderingly. 'Heaven alone knows why I haven't done so,' she sighed.

'Then I'd better kiss you again before you set off with all bells ringing.'

But before he could do so the faint sound of voices floated to their ears, warning them that people were coming up the hill. Leon stood up abruptly, his hand outstretched to pull Sara to her feet. 'There'll be another time,' he promised in a low voice.

'I—I'm not sure there should be,' Sara returned, conscious of disappointment as they made their way down the hill.

Leon shrugged, his attitude so casual that by the time they reached the car the kiss on the hill seemed to have evaporated into a dream so remote that Sara wondered if it had really happened. Well, it had better not happen again, she decided firmly, otherwise she'd become like putty in his hands, as Iris Radcliffe had warned.

Nor was there any need to fool herself into believing it had had no effect on her. She had enjoyed the undeniable thrill, and if she was not careful it could become a habit which would develop into something from which there could be no return.

It would be safer to rid herself of the memory, she resolved, again reminding herself that it had been only part of Leon's purpose and a means to an end. Yet, strangely, she had sensed protection in the feel of his arms about her body, and perhaps it was this element which had caused her to respond with such ardour to his embrace.

'Ready for lunch?' she asked casually while spreading a rug in the shade of a lakefront poplar tree.

'Starving.' The reply came in a tone that was vaguely abrupt.

He lifted the hamper from the car, placed it on the rug and they settled themselves on either side of it. They ate in what at first appeared to be companionable silence until it dawned on Sara that Leon had little to say.

Instinct suggested that he was thinking about their recent kiss on the hill, and, sending covert glances towards his face, she saw that his brow had darkened while he stared across the water through narrowed lids. 'The food is not to your liking?' she queried.

'Good grief, what makes you ask such a question?'

'Your face. It wears a look of suppressed annoyance.'

He said nothing.

'It betrays an inner irritation,' she persisted. 'Perhaps you're regretting those—those moments of closeness?' Somehow she had to know about this.

'If that's what you think, you're entirely mistaken,' he told her.

She ignored his denial by going on relentlessly, 'If you *are* regretting those moments, they needn't bother you. You can forget them—as I certainly shall.'

'Just as you've forgotten the kisses Purvis showered all over your face? Or *haven't* you forgotten them?' His mouth twisted as he snapped the latter question.

'Terry?' Sara sat up abruptly to stare at him. 'What has he to do with this discussion?'

'If you must know, he came into my mind while I was kissing you. I thought, *Purvis did this*, and it made me mad,' he snarled.

She gaped at him incredulously. Could he be hinting that he was jealous of Terry? No, it was merely his subtle way of persuading her along the path towards his goal, which, of course, was his plan for their property.

Their property. It was the first time she had thought of it as being in joint ownership, and, annoyed by her own submission, she said crossly, 'Apart from intruding into my home, must you also intrude into my past?'

'Yes—though only the devil knows why,' he admitted frankly, the scowl again returning to his face.

Her chin rose as she declared loftily, 'Then hear this— I am not even remotely interested in *your* past. I couldn't care less about the number of girls you've kissed.'

'No? OK, I won't give it another thought.'

'Good. Now perhaps you'll try to enjoy your lunch.' The suggestion was uttered in a tone of forced levity as she thought about his recent words. *Him?* Jealous of Terry? That was a laugh!

They ate the meal in what could only be termed a strained silence until Leon dabbed at his lips with a paper napkin, then lay back on the rug. 'You haven't spoken for at least ten minutes,' he drawled, staring up at the quivering leaves above their heads. 'Does this mean you're the sulky type?'

'No, it does not,' she snapped, dragging her eyes away from the muscular contours of his long form. 'I was merely pondering about the Jekyll and Hyde type of man who holds a girl closely, then insults her a short time later. I've no intention of living with such a man.'

'No? So what will you do about it?' he queried lazily and without bothering to turn his head.

'I'll appeal to Mr Abernethy. I—I'll tell him my life is being made a misery and—and that he must do something about you.'

'That should give him a good laugh,' he chuckled. 'Especially when I tell him about your response to my kisses, and the lovely feel of your arms round my neck.'

'You wouldn't!' she exclaimed, appalled by the thought of those private moments being discussed, probably with amusement.

'Try me and see for yourself,' Leon warned grimly.

'But that's blackmail!'

'An ugly word to come from lips as sweet as your own. I prefer to look on it as a means to an end.'

'Exactly. The end of the cottage. At least you admit it.' Her words rang with accusation.

He sat up abruptly and stared at her, his face inscrutable. 'Doesn't it occur to you that the end I have in mind could be something entirely different?'

A scornful laugh escaped her. 'Different from the demolition of the cottage? If you imagine you've got me fooled you're mistaken, Leon Longley. I know those moments of—of closeness meant nothing to you, and if you think a few kisses will place me in the palm of your hand you've got another think coming!'

'You're beginning to sound like a shrew,' he observed coolly.

'Thank you very much!' she snapped furiously, then began packing the hamper before tears of anger could fill her eyes.

Watching her, he murmured, 'Pity the poor plates. Even plastic has its limits.'

She controlled the force she was using, then remarked in an abrupt tone, 'Didn't you say there were various areas you wanted to examine for—*development*? Perhaps we should get on with it.'

'They can wait. At the moment I've lost the urge. Even Kinloch has lost its appeal.' His own tone had become morose.

Sara spoke coldly. 'Then let's go home before you're subjected to further—er—shrewishness.' The outing had been ruined, she realised, mainly by herself.

It was mid-afternoon before they left Kinloch, and as they drove back towards Taupo their former amicable relationship reasserted itself. The scowl left Leon's face, and Sara found herself laughing at his droll comments. Nor did she fail to appreciate that his humour was aimed at lifting her own spirits.

When they reached home he carried the hamper into the kitchen and lifted the lid. 'There's not much food left,' he remarked. 'We'll go out to dinner.'

'There's no need,' she assured him. 'There are TV dinners in the freezer. I'll put a couple in the oven.'

'OK, I'll check that we have pre-dinner drinks.'

She dealt with the remaining contents of the hamper, then went to the living-room, where she found him examining the array of bottles in the cabinet. One by one they were held to the light to check the amounts left in them.

Glancing at her, he said, 'Some are almost empty. I'll attend to replacing them.'

'That's not necessary——' she began.

'Of course it's necessary. I've no intention of allowing you to pay for my evening pre-dinner drinks.'

Sara looked at him mutely while the words sank in to remind her that he really did intend to take up residence in Rosemary Cottage. To confirm it she said, 'So you definitely are moving in?'

He laughed. 'Does a man fill the cellar, then move off and leave it? Besides, you're forgetting I've made arrangements with Edith Sellwood.'

She took a glass of sherry from him, then admitted, 'For the moment I had forgotten. The situation seems so unreal.'

'You still want her to come?' His tone was soft while he watched her narrowly.

'Yes, of course. If you're definitely staying we must have another woman here.'

'That's right—you mustn't be compromised,' he agreed gravely.

Another sherry kept Sara feeling cheerful and enabled the evening to be passed in amicable friendship. The covers taken off the heated TV dinners released appetising aromas, and they ate while watching the news. But although she tried to concentrate her thoughts kept drifting away to those moments on the hill at Kinloch.

In an effort to see them more clearly she closed her eyes to shut out the TV screen, then the feel of Leon's hand on her arm indicated that he was watching her. 'Something tells me you're almost asleep,' she heard him say.

She opened her eyes and smiled apologetically. 'I had a restless night, and I've had a long day. Nor am I accustomed to climbing hills——' She stopped, regretting those last words.

'Nor to being kissed at the top of them?' The question came in a low deep voice.

'Isn't that something we'd be wise to forget?' she asked shakily.

'I've no intention of doing so.' The words came abruptly.

A look of strain crossed her face as a wave of weariness overcame her. 'I'm afraid you'll have to excuse me—I really must go to bed,' she muttered, rising unsteadily to her feet while fatigue caused her to almost stumble.

Leon was beside her in an instant, his enfolding arms causing her to lean against him. 'You look as if you're about to drop where you stand,' he remarked in a tone that betrayed sympathy.

Sara revelled in the comfort of his nearness, and while she reminded herself that this was something she had every intention of avoiding, she was unable to find the energy to push him away. At least, she told herself she lacked the energy until a burst of honesty forced her to admit she had no wish to push him away.

There was a feeling of sweet security in the strength of the arms that held her, a gentleness in the hand that moved to stroke her head as it rested against his shoulder.

The fingers that tilted her chin were firm, forcing her to meet his penetrating gaze.

Her eyes closed as his lips trailed from her brow to her lids, then slid down the silky softness of her cheek to find her mouth. His sensuous nibbling, coupled with the pressure of his body against her own, plunged her mind into a state of confusion which held her hovering between what she should do, and the abandoned response she longed to make.

It was a kiss that seemed to go on for ever, and as his body moved gently against her own she became vitally aware of his arousal. And while the knowledge that he wanted her gave her a feeling of triumph, she also knew she must grasp at control. Her fingers ceased to fondle the hair at the nape of his neck, and her arms found their way to push against his chest.

Her protest came as a muffled murmur. 'Leon, please—no more. This is ridiculous!'

He made no move to release her. 'That's not what I'd call it.'

'Well, it can't go on,' she said firmly.

He looked down into her face. 'You're afraid of me?'

She was unable to meet his eyes. 'Yes, a little.'

'You're afraid I'll come to your bedroom and demand more than my half share of the cottage?'

Sara buried her face against his chest while she nodded.

'I can assure you there's no need for apprehension.'

'Nevertheless I'll lock the door,' she mumbled.

'Don't trouble. I shan't come to your room.'

'That's a promise?' she demanded anxiously.

'Definitely. Wild horses wouldn't drag me there.'

She raised her face to look up at him in silence, her mind confused. He could kiss her with such passion, yet had no desire to make love with her? She had felt positive he wanted her, but now his words came like a shower of crushed ice. They seemed strangely inconsistent—nor was she sure whether to be relieved or bitterly disappointed.

CHAPTER SIX

NEXT morning gave promise of another warm day, and when Sara came into the kitchen Leon ran appreciative eyes over her chic yet severe navy and white suit.

'You're looking very businesslike,' he observed. 'But of course, you have an appointment with our mutual friend.'

She avoided looking at him by sprinkling cornflakes over the peaches she intended having for breakfast, and as she sat down she admitted, 'It's certainly time I visited Mr Abernethy. By failing to do so I've probably earned any shocks I've received.'

'I'm glad you recognise that small fact,' he murmured.

She finished her breakfast without further comment, and by the time she left the house she was gripped by impatience to get the matter settled—at least in her own mind.

Nor did she miss the twinkle in John Abernethy's blue eyes as he ushered her into his office. It told her that the slim elderly man was secretly amused, which was proved when he sat behind his desk and spoke in a dry tone.

'Am I right in assuming you've been somewhat—rocked?'

'Rocked is an understatement,' Sara declared vehemently.

'At the funeral I hinted that you should come to see me as soon as possible, remember?'

She nodded. 'Yes, I—I should have come earlier,' Sara admitted.

'I expected to see you the next day.' He paused while long fingers stroked his neatly clipped grey beard, then

94

he went on without further preamble, 'Ah, so he's arrived?'

Sara nodded again. There was no need to ask to whom he referred. 'And what's more, he's moved in!' she exclaimed, her indignation bursting forth. 'Is it possible for you to explain this situation to me, Mr Abernethy?'

He stared at her in silence for several long moments before he said, 'When some people grow older they do strange things with their wills.'

'But not people like Jane,' Sara stated firmly.

'Even Mrs Patterson made a will that held a surprise.'

Sara decided the situation called for bluntness. 'But she always promised that the property would be mine,' she declared flatly.

Mr Abernethy sighed. 'Yes, I believe you. Her previous will states that simple fact, yet during November she sat in that very chair, full of purpose and her mind made up about what should happen to that part of her estate known as Rosemary Cottage.'

'She never said a word to me about this—this man. I don't even recall her mentioning his name,' Sara said morosely. 'It must have been an impulsive decision.'

John Abernethy looked at her kindly. 'I'll admit I thought it was a strange whim, so I asked if she'd given it sufficient consideration. She was quite adamant about having done so.'

'Yet she gave no indication as to her reason?'

He frowned. 'She muttered something about Samuel, her late husband. It seemed she'd been worrying over what Samuel would have wished her to do. After all, her entire estate had come to her through him, and I can only assume she felt guilty about excluding every member of his family.'

Sara looked at him blankly, unable to find anything to say while suspecting the solicitor's surmise to be correct. She knew that her great-aunt's thoughts had never been far from the memory of Samuel, and it was easy to believe that the thought of Rosemary Cottage going out of his family had begun to niggle at her conscience.

'Had you quarrelled with her?' John Abernethy's question came bluntly.

Sara shook her head. 'There was never a cross word between us.'

'She was never critical of you?' he probed. 'Older people are very good at finding fault with the younger generation.'

Again Sara shook her head. 'Her only criticism was my lack of social life. I—I don't go out very often—I mean during the evening.' She paused, then recalled, 'Great-Aunt Jane used to declare that if I was determined to be an old maid I had no need to live like one before the time came.'

'Ah, is that a fact?' The blue eyes narrowed thoughtfully as they looked at her across the desk.

'So what am I to do, Mr Abernethy?' The question came plaintively.

'In the meantime, do nothing,' he advised.

'I mean about getting this man out of *my house*!'

'But it's not your house. Half of it belongs to Leon Longley. In any case, nothing can be done until probate has been granted, and until then you'd be wise to make the best of the situation.'

'And let the neighbours talk? Mrs Next Door is having a wonderful time at her kitchen window!'

The solicitor laughed. 'Why worry about her? She's probably jealous of you, and with plenty to be envious about, I'd say.'

Sara hesitated, then admitted, 'Well, actually, Leon has arranged for an older woman to come and stay with us.' She went on to tell him of the little she knew about Edith Sellwood.

'A friend of Leon's mother, you say? She sounds very suitable,' John Abernethy commented. 'However, you'll probably find that most of Leon's time will be spent in the Auckland office.'

'But he spoke of opening an office in Taupo——' Sara began.

'He might open one, but you'll find he'll put an agent in it because, as he's head of the firm, his place is in Auckland.'

Sara felt doubtful. 'I'm not so sure about that. Leon Longley is a determined man, and something tells me that his place will be wherever he wants it to be. What's more, he likes Taupo.'

'Getting to know him well, are you?' An amused note crept into the elderly man's voice as he added, 'Perhaps he also likes what he's discovered at Taupo.'

Sara ignored the insinuation as she asked, 'So there's nothing I can do about preventing him from entering the house?'

'You're forgetting that Mrs Patterson left a key in my possession—a key to be given to him in the event of her death. That fact alone indicates her wishes.' The solicitor stared at the desk for several moments before sending her a penetrating stare. 'Have you any thoughts of contesting this will?'

She felt shocked by the suggestion. 'Contest Jane's will? Oh, no, I wouldn't dream of fighting against her wishes to that extent, especially after she's been more than generous to me. It's just that I don't know how to cope with her wishes.'

The solicitor looked sympathetic. 'Just give it time to sort itself out,' he advised. 'Hasten slowly, as the saying goes, and if the time comes when you can no longer tolerate this man's presence in the house we'll talk again. We'll see what other arrangements can be made.'

Sara swallowed but said nothing as she stared at the papers on the desk. A sudden flash of memory put Leon's arms around her, while honesty compelled her to admit she had moved several steps from being unable to tolerate his presence in the house. Further, she was thankful that Mr Abernethy could not read her thoughts, because her mind had evolved into a confused mass of stupid contradictions—one moment wanting Leon out of the house, while the next instant she longed for him to stay in it. There was an exhilarating quality in his company, she admitted to herself—something that caused her pulses to quicken.

'Hasten slowly,' the solicitor repeated, watching her face. 'You might find value in having a man about the house, and, as Mrs Patterson tried to do as Samuel would have wished, it's up to you to do as she—er—obviously desired.'

Again refusing to listen to the insinuation in his voice, Sara said, 'I can at least take care of the herb garden, but if Leon wants to pull down the cottage and build flats I'll fight him.'

'Worry about that when—and if—he makes that decision,' John Abernethy advised, shuffling through papers. 'In the meantime you might like to learn the extent of your changed financial circumstances.'

She looked at him in silence. Was he deliberately changing the subject? Suspicion that he knew more than he had admitted about Jane's wishes began to nag at her mind, but these thoughts were overridden as she sat listening to the details of her legacy. 'Are you saying my great-aunt left me so much?' she asked at last.

'That's right. The contents of the cottage will belong to you, plus all her personal items, jewellery, and the income from various investments. She never did live up to all she received. However, there'll be tax to pay.'

'And the cottage to be maintained,' Sara put in, a stubborn note creeping into her voice. 'Soon it will need to be painted.'

'That expense will now be shared,' he reminded her.

'Which is half the trouble. I'm sure Leon will consider it to be money down the drain,' she said resentfully.

'He could be right,' the solicitor pointed out. 'You'll be shocked by today's cost of painting those old timbers.'

Sara's expression became obstinate. 'I promised it would be maintained, and that promise I intend to keep.'

'Ah yes, but that was when you understood the cottage would belong to you entirely. Those circumstances have now changed, and in all fairness you must look at it from Leon's point of view.'

She bit her lower lip, waiting for him to remind her of points already creeping into her own thoughts.

He went on, regarding her kindly. 'You must remember that your sense of responsibility is fired by sentiment, as well as a promise made to your great-aunt. But you must also remember that this man Leon Longley is a virtual stranger to the situation. He has little sentiment for that old cottage, nor did he make any promises to a person who was somewhat far removed in the field of in-laws.'

'I suppose you're right,' Sara admitted with reluctance.

'If he becomes a permanent resident in the house its maintenance will be of value to him; but if he does not, the cost of its upkeep will be of value only to you.'

'Yes, I can understand that point.'

'For him it will be, as you said, money down the drain.'

Her chin rose while she spoke with an air of determination. 'Nevertheless I shall spend whatever money is necessary, whether or not he pays his share. Jane maintained it in memory of Samuel, and I shall maintain it in memory of her.'

The solicitor looked at her in thoughtful silence until he said, 'I can't help wondering whether you aim to own that old cottage, or whether it already owns you.'

She stood up, smiling at him. 'Only time will tell, Mr Abernethy, but in the meantime one thing is certain. Leon Longley will not sway me from carrying out Jane's wishes.'

The solicitor's eyes were shrewd. 'Her wishes—ah, yes, I'd like to know a little more about those same wishes— as if I can't guess,' he added in a muttered undertone.

Sara brushed the comment aside as she held out her hand and said, 'It's time I returned to the salon.

Goodbye, and thank you for your advice.' Nor was there time for the employment agency, she realised.

'The salon keeps you busy, apparently,' he remarked.

She ignored the reminder of her tardiness in visiting him, and instead she explained, 'We're almost fully booked for this afternoon, and for the rest of the week.'

'Well, come and see me if you have any *real* problems,' he advised.

She felt irritated. 'You don't think this is a real problem?'

'It doesn't sound too serious to me,' he smiled.

Sara held back a retort about men always sticking together, and when she returned to the salon she found she had not exaggerated. The place was indeed busy, with women sitting beneath the hairdryers, while one awaited attention in a chair near the desk. Pam was busy winding rollers on to hair that was being permed, while Dawn was occupied with blow-waving a mop of brilliant red hair.

Sara went to the staff-room, where she changed into her uniform, and as she did so she turned to find Dawn beside her.

The latter's eyes were troubled as she said in a low voice, 'This blow-wave didn't have an appointment. She's a casual who walked in and demanded to be done by the senior assistant. I'm afraid she's in a very bad mood—quite cross, in fact. *Please* take over.'

Sara's brows rose. 'Why? You always do a good job.'

'I'm doing my best, but when I told her you were out and that I could do her she looked me up and down, then said she supposed she'd have to risk it. I felt like telling her to go hopping sideways, but I'm not in the habit of turning away business.'

Sara smiled. 'You were right. Did you get her name?'

'Yes, it's in the book.'

'OK, I'll finish her while you shampoo Mrs Briggs.'

'You'll find her manners don't match the pretty face and lovely hair,' warned Dawn.

Sara went to the appointment book to learn the identity of the difficult client, then found she could only stare at the name as though unable to decipher the letters. *Sellwood?* Could this be Edith Sellwood? She turned to look at the woman who sat draped by the protective pink and grey cover. No, this person was too young to be Edith Sellwood. She just happened to have the same name, and, looking at the book again, Sara realised that this was *Miss* Sellwood.

As she approached the chair the client's voice spoke coldly. 'I'm thankful my blow-wave is to be continued— *at last.*'

'Unavoidable delay,' Sara said with deliberate cheerfulness while meeting a pair of green eyes in the mirror.

The client's voice remained cool. 'I presume you're the *senior* assistant?'

'Yes.' Sara's reply came from compressed lips.

'Well, at least that's something. I happen to be accustomed to having my hair done in a large Auckland salon, and always by the head girl. I find the juniors to be so inefficient,' the woman added in a scathing tone. 'Nor am I amused to find myself being attended to by the junior in a small crummy dump in Taupo—— She stopped abruptly, perhaps realising her lack of tact.

Sara took a deep breath, then spoke calmly. 'There's nothing inefficient about Dawn's work. However, if you're not satisfied with the way she's been blow-waving your hair perhaps you'd feel happier if you left now and found a different salon.' She laid down the roller brush, switched off the hand-dryer and began to remove the cover, each action holding deliberate purpose.

Miss Sellwood gaped at her in the mirror. 'You mean you'd turn me out half finished?'

'That's right. I don't have to tolerate rudeness, nor this salon being referred to as a crummy dump.'

The woman twisted in her chair to stare at Sara, her indignation turning to dismay as she realised that Sara meant what she said. 'I'm sorry, I'm afraid the words

just slipped out. Mummy says I should watch my tongue,
but it's just that I'm so anxious to look nice for this—
this special occasion.'

'Then you should have had your hair done in
Auckland by the head girl,' Sara told her frankly, still
feeling ruffled.

'Unfortunately she was busy,' Miss Sellwood admitted. 'And I'm afraid I was in a hurry to reach Taupo.'

'For this special occasion?' queried Sara, her curiosity beginning to nag at her despite her effort to
maintain the usual impersonal relationship she held towards clients.

Miss Sellwood smiled winningly as she pleaded, '*Please*
do my hair. You see, I shall be staying with my fiancé,
and I must look my best for him.'

'Oh, so you're engaged to be married?'

'Well, not yet—but it should be announced before very
long—especially as I'll be living alone with him.' She
favoured Sara with a knowing look, then gazed down at
the slender fingers of her left hand, almost as if already
seeing an enhancing sparkle on one of them.

Sara replaced the cover about the slim shoulders and
finished the blow-wave. She took particular care with
the job, and as she played the hand-dryer on the roller
brush she longed to ask questions but would not permit
herself to do so.

Mummy says—— Was this girl with the beautiful face
and hair Megan Sellwood, the daughter of Edith? Had
Edith already arrived, bringing her daughter with her—
and was Edith as arrogant as her daughter? But most
important of all, was Leon the prospective fiancé?

Strangely, the thought gave Sara a pain until she
realised she must be mistaken, because this person would
not be living alone with him. She herself would be there,
as well as Edith Sellwood.

But then further doubts raised their heads as the client
said with a hint of satisfaction, 'My fiancé has recently
inherited a house on the lakefront.'

'Really? How nice for you both.' It was all Sara could think of to say while becoming conscious of her own sinking spirits. And then her depression switched to anger as Miss Sellwood went on in an offhand manner.

'Of course all the lakefront land is really valuable, although I suspect the house to be little better than a crummy old cottage. I dare say it'll have to be demolished and replaced by something much more modern— *ouch*, that *hurt*! You pulled my hair! I shan't come back to this salon again.'

Sara sent her a smile of forced sweetness as she said, 'I can only hope you'll keep *that* promise.'

Miss Sellwood glared at her via the mirror. 'My goodness, I find you too independent for words. I've a good mind to report you to the owner of this place!'

Sara spoke coldly. 'You do that. The opportunity might come sooner than you think.'

Nothing further was said while she finished the wave with all possible speed. Nor was she sorry to see this particular client leave the salon, especially as she was now convinced that this was Edith Sellwood's daughter. Hadn't Leon said that Edith had been a beautiful redhead in her younger days? But had he really referred to Jane's bequest as a crummy old cottage? No—that was one of *her* favourite words.

The rest of the afternoon found Sara plagued by thoughts of Edith Sellwood and her daughter, and although she tried to concentrate on light conversation while winding rollers for a perm, her mind kept slipping away towards Rosemary Cottage.

The strong urge to go home grew upon her steadily, yet she forced herself to remain at the job until late in the afternoon when she was able to hand over the finishing stages and brushing out of sets to Dawn and Pam.

Apprehension sat heavily on her as she drove along the lakefront, and as she turned into the drive the sight of a small car occupying her own garage space came as no surprise. It seemed to nestle beside the Daimler, causing her to wonder if this could be an omen of further nestling to come.

Irritated, she left her own car in a sheltered area at the back of the house, then went into the kitchen, where she was brought to a standstill by the sound of a female voice floating from the living-room. Nor was this the first time she'd heard those same petulant tones.

'Mummy knew you'd be sure to understand her situation.'

Something like the sound of a grunt came in Leon's voice.

Sara did not wait to hear more, and without further hesitation she walked into the living-room, where she found herself faced by the woman who had earlier been in the salon. And again she was struck by the fieriness of her hair, especially with the late afternoon sun glinting on it through the window.

The sight of Sara brought Megan Sellwood to her feet, her green eyes widening to stare incredulously as she exclaimed, 'Good grief, it's the woman from the salon! What the devil are *you* doing here?'

'I live here,' Sara informed her coolly.

'You—are living here—*with Leon*? I don't believe you.'

Sara's shoulders moved slightly as she turned to Leon. 'Haven't you told her about the situation between us?'

The green eyes were suddenly narrowed as Megan hissed, 'What situation? What are you talking about?'

A faint smile flickered about Leon's mobile lips as he raised a dark brow at Sara. 'Am I to understand you've already met Megan?'

'Oh, yes, we've met.' The words came grimly.

Megan said petulantly, 'She did my hair in that crummy salon——'

Sara rose to the attack. 'Don't you *dare* call my salon crummy!' she snapped furiously.

Megan's eyes widened. 'Your salon? You mean you *own* it?'

'That's right. And you're one of the most unpleasant clients to have stepped into it!'

Leon broke in hastily while making a move towards the drinks cabinet, 'Watch it, girls—we don't want quarrels. Let's have a sherry to wipe away whatever rancour is simmering between you.'

But Sara was not yet ready for peace, and, still fired by anger, she turned on him, her voice accusing. 'I understand that *you* have referred to this place as a *crummy old cottage*. Well now, there's gratitude for you! I'm glad Jane didn't hear you. She loved this place and would have been very hurt.'

His jaw tightened as he demanded curtly, 'Who the hell told you that nonsense?'

She sent him a level glance. 'Need you ask?' Then before he could deny the charge she went on in a tone that was full of resentment, 'Incidentally, am I not due for an explanation? Correct me if my imagination has been playing tricks, but I understood that an older person had been engaged to come here.'

He handed her a glass of sherry. 'I was about to hear an explanation when you arrived home—and then the fireworks began.'

'You're blaming me for defending my salon?' Sara demanded with indignation.

'Never mind your salon,' Megan cut in impatiently. 'I was merely explaining to Leon that Mummy couldn't come. He'd phoned and told her he needed to spend time in a house he'd inherited, and he needed someone to care for him.'

'I'm afraid *Mummy* got it wrong,' Leon put in sardonically. 'But then Mummy often does,' he added with a touch of weariness.

Megan ignored his last words as she said, 'The situation is that Mummy hadn't quite finished the job of caring for an elderly man whose people are away on holiday, so she sent me in her place.'

'You were free to do this?' asked Sara. 'You don't normally hold down a regular job?'

'Of course I have a job,' Megan told her loftily. 'I work in my father's office, but he gave me the time off to come to Leon. Daddy knew it was imperative because we mean so much to each other,' she added, sending Leon a smile that was full of confidence.

Sara swept a glance from Megan to Leon. 'Of course, I understand perfectly—especially after the information you gave me in the salon. I mean about your—er—very close association with him.'

Megan flushed. 'Well, actually, not all of that was exactly true. I mean, you should be able to under-stand——'

The confession amazed Sara. 'Are you admitting you were handing me a load of exaggeration?'

'I suppose you could call it that—but it's only tem-porary, if you get my meaning. It'll all come right in the end.'

Leon sent a puzzled glance from Sara to Megan. 'Would one of you be good enough to tell me what you're going on about?'

Sara began to laugh as she caught the flash of appeal in Megan's eyes. It caused her to take pity on her, so she refrained from saying *so he's not your fiancé after all*. For some inexplicable reason she was merely thankful to learn it was not a fact—at least not yet, even if Megan's parents were doing their best to hasten the project into becoming a reality.

Leon refilled their glasses. 'Perhaps another sherry will help loosen your tongues sufficiently to explain these enigmatic remarks,' he said drily.

Sara took several sips, then stared thoughtfully into the golden liquid until at last she said, 'Leon, it seems to me that the explanation should come from you to

Megan. She appears to have an incorrect picture of the situation between us.'

Megan spoke quickly. 'Oh, yes, this situation between you—I want to hear about that. It sounds as if it could be something I should know about,' she added with a hint of suspicion, her eyes darting from Leon to Sara.

He shrugged. 'It's quite simple.'

A short laugh escaped Sara. 'Simple? Is it, indeed? You're ignoring all the problems lurking in the background.'

He regarded her mildly, his brows raised. 'Problems?' he queried.

Sara sent him a singularly sweet smile. 'You know exactly what I'm talking about, so don't try to deny——'

Megan broke in impatiently, 'So what is she talking about? You must tell me at once, Leon—you owe it to me.'

He turned to her with a sigh of resignation. 'Get this straight, Megan, I owe you nothing. However, the truth is that Sara and I share the inheritance of this property. It's a joint ownership.'

Megan's jaw sagged slightly. 'But does that mean she has to live here? Has she the right to move in?'

Sara's indignation began to get the better of her. 'I've lived here for four years,' she snapped. 'Leon is the intruder. It's he who has no need to be here.' The last words ended with a glare at the tall man who stood regarding her with amusement.

Megan looked at Leon, her eyes almost pleading. 'If you have equal shares, shouldn't you, being the man, say who's to live in this house?'

He laughed. 'You're about two hundred years out of date, Megan.'

She went on petulantly, 'But Mummy said you *needed* me, so you must have had ideas of putting her out.'

'Putting me out?' Sara gasped at the audacity of the suggestion. 'You've got a confounded nerve!' she snapped at Megan, then swung round to face Leon. 'Or is this what you really had in mind?'

'Don't be stupid,' he snarled, then turned to Megan with a snort of impatience. 'I'm afraid *Mummy* doesn't appear to have latched on to what I was trying to explain during our phone conversation. But that's not surprising, because she talks on and on without taking in what the other person is trying to say.'

'Mummy isn't like that,' Megan protested.

'You know perfectly well that she *is* like that,' Leon persisted frankly. 'You're so accustomed to it you don't seem to notice that she gets her tongue into top gear and continues non-stop.'

'Well, yes, perhaps she does go on a bit,' Megan conceded. 'I'll admit Daddy says her constant yakking drives him up the wall—but believe me, she knows exactly what's being said, and what she herself has in mind.'

A sudden gleam appeared in Leon's eyes. 'Yes, by Jove, you're probably right about that point. However, the situation is that Sara feels we need another woman in the house—an older woman, for the sake of propriety, you understand.'

The dimples in Megan's cheeks came and went. 'How very quaint! Her mind must be back in the past—like two hundred years out of date,' she flashed at him.

He ignored the indirect taunt at Sara as he went on, 'This woman would be a housekeeper who'd take care of all that's to be done, and she'd also attend to our meals.' His expression changed to an amused grin. 'Somehow I can't see you giving up your softly cushioned job with Daddy to take on such a situation.'

Megan moved to stand closer to him, the dimples again flashing as her eyes gazed up at him soulfully. When she spoke the words came in a quietly serious tone. 'Leon, you and I have known each other since childhood. You know I'm very fond of you, and you're well aware that I'll do anything for you. I'll wash and cook and take care of you—but if you think I'll act as *her* housekeeper while she's dancing about in her crummy salon, you have another think coming. So—either *she* goes or I go. Is it understood?'

His mouth twisted into a mirthless grin. 'My goodness, that's quite a speech! It reminds me of Mummy.'

'But is it understood?' Megan persisted.

'Yes, Megan, it's understood,' Leon said. 'Obviously the job isn't suitable for you.'

'Wrong,' Sara was goaded to cut in. 'It's the other way round. Megan isn't suitable for the job. Nor have I any intention of seeing it filled by a person who constantly refers to my business as a crummy salon. *Is that understood?*'

He frowned. 'Yes, of course, but I'm sure Megan didn't mean to be hurtful.'

'Didn't she? She could have fooled me.' Sara's tone was scathing, then she took a deep breath as she said, 'Incidentally, there's another small point you appear to be overlooking.'

Leon sent her a sharp glance. 'Oh? What would that be?'

'The matter of choosing the person to live with us is not entirely in your hands. I also have a say in it.'

'Yes, I suppose that's right,' he conceded.

Sara went on, 'As far as I'm concerned Megan's rude attitude puts her right at the bottom of the list, so I shall go to the employment agency. I'm sure they'll find someone for us—someone with whom we can both feel compatible.'

'OK, you do that,' Leon agreed on a weary note. 'Perhaps it would be better. I can see there's no hope of you two girls getting together on friendly terms.' He turned to Megan and added, 'It's a pity your journey appears to have been for nothing.'

Megan swallowed but remained silent for several moments. She moved to the window, where she stood staring across the lake, then she turned and said quickly, 'Actually, we could get on well together, because Sara would

scarcely be here. She'd be away all day in her—er—salon.
We'd see so little of each other, and—and eventually we
might come to—to know each other better.'

Sara spoke in a dull voice. 'I'm not interested in
knowing you better, Megan. You've already given me a
very clear picture of yourself, and I can't say I'm
impressed.'

'But can't we try?' pleaded Megan. 'Nobody would
take care of Leon as well as myself,' she added naïvely.

'Then the poor fellow will have to make an effort to
take care of himself, or put up with whoever we find,'
Sara retorted, aghast to hear the sarcasm dripping from
her own lips.

Megan clasped her hands as she appealed to Leon.
'Can't you make her see that we need this opportunity
to be together?'

'Do we?' His tone was harsh.

'Of course we do—you *know* we do——' she pleaded.

Sara looked at him curiously, wondering about the
coolness that had crept into his attitude. Was it directed
at Megan or towards herself? Did he really want to have
Megan living in the house? Perhaps, if she gave them
the opportunity to be together, it would settle the
question one way or the other.

She looked at Megan, sensing her desperate search for
further pleading words, then her own reluctant words
were dragged from her. 'Very well, you two shall have
the chance to be together all day. You'll be able to recount childhood memories about playing hide and seek,
kiss-in-the-ring, or whatever.'

'You'll agree to give it a trial period?' asked Leon,
ignoring her bantering remarks.

Again Sara regarded him curiously. Had she detected
a note of relief in his voice? 'What sort of period would
you have in mind?' she asked cautiously.

Megan spoke quickly. 'Daddy said he'll give me a
fortnight to—to——' The words died on her lips.

'To clinch the deal?' Sara asked frankly. She was still feeling irritated by Megan's slur on her salon and wondered why she was being sufficiently stupid to allow this woman into the house.

She turned to look at Leon, and was startled to discover him regarding her with a strange expression on his face—one she found impossible to fathom. Was it mocking, or was it questioning? Did he wonder if she could be merely acting in defiance through jealousy of Megan? If so she'd let him know she couldn't care less regarding his relationship with the beautiful redhead, so she sent him a lofty glance as she said, 'If Megan is willing to hold out the hand of friendship, I'm quite capable of doing likewise. OK, we'll give it a trial.'

The frown left his brow. 'Good girl! I felt sure you'd be reasonable.'

'Reasonable? Me? Huh!' Watching him closely, she again thought he appeared to be relieved.

'I mean under the circumstances, and considering you expected the arrival of an older woman,' he explained.

Sara felt a sudden depression. He wants Megan to be here, she decided, irritated by the knowledge, and this suspicion seemed to be confirmed by his next words.

'In any case, she would have to stay here tonight because at this hour I wouldn't allow her to set out on the long drive home to Auckland,' he declared firmly.

A sigh of relief escaped Megan. 'Dear Leon, you were always so thoughtful towards me!' she cooed, gazing up at him.

Watching him, Sara was struck by the fact that he definitely had Megan's welfare at heart, and again she was assailed by a surge of peevishness. But further irritation was to come.

'Well, that's settled,' Megan said happily, then, turning to Sara, she announced inconsequently, 'I know where I'm to sleep. I've already been through the rooms and have put my suitcase in the front bedroom. It'll suit me nicely.'

Sara was jolted into realising she had not given a thought to this question, mainly because she had not expected to be faced by it quite so soon. But now she uttered a quick protest that echoed her dismay. 'You're not sleeping in Jane's room!'

'Why not?' Megan pouted. 'I want that room.'

'You're not sleeping in there because I say so,' Sara snapped.

Leon gave a snort of derision. 'So much for the hand of friendship!' he rasped, his disapproval directed towards Sara.

CHAPTER SEVEN

MEGAN appealed to Leon, 'What's wrong with her? Has she gone potty?'

Sara ignored the remark as she also appealed to Leon, 'Can't you make her understand that it's my great-aunt's room?'

'So what?' demanded Megan in an amused tone.

Leon's disapproval vanished, his manner more gentle as he spoke to Sara. 'Are you forgetting that Jane is no longer here?'

'Of course I'm not forgetting,' she flung at him. 'But you must remember that her clothes are still here. All her personal odds and ends are still in the room, which is just as she left it. Do you think she'd want a stranger poking and prying among her things?' Sara was perilously near tears.

Leon continued to speak quietly. 'Aren't you overreacting?'

'No, I am not!' Sara retorted vehemently. 'You must understand that I have to deal with all the things in that room, but the thought of finding homes for them makes me feel I'm pushing Jane even further away.'

'She couldn't be further away than by death,' Megan cut in heartlessly.

'Shut up, Megan!' snarled Leon. 'You're talking like a tactless idiot. If you don't watch your tongue you're likely to find yourself out on your neck.'

'I was only being realistic,' Megan protested. 'Jane's things should have been dealt with straight after the funeral.'

'No, no, I couldn't bear to do that!' The words were wrung from Sara like a wail of distress.

113

'Rubbish,' snapped Megan. 'You just force yourself to do what you've got to do.'

Leon said, 'Megan, you're not only stupid, you're as hard as flint. I must say you really surprise me.'

She turned to him swiftly. 'You know that's not true. You know I'm a loving, caring person, otherwise I wouldn't be here.' Then, swinging round to face Sara, she demanded impatiently, 'So—in which of those three bedrooms am I to sleep?'

'You will occupy my room,' Sara told her. 'I shall change the bed linen and carry my belongings into Jane's room.'

Megan made an appeal to Leon. 'Can't you make her see sense? *I want the end room!*'

'Where's your own common sense?' The words were uttered in a low growl. 'It's for Sara to say where you'll sleep. Anyhow, why are you so set on occupying that particular room?'

Megan turned sulky, again appealing to him like a spoilt child. 'Leon dear, you know what my room at home is like. It's a mere box, whereas this is a lovely sunny room with a wonderful view. I—I've set my heart on it, so please talk to her about it.'

Sara felt a small twist of inner pain as she sent a frank glance towards Leon. 'So you know what her room at home is like. How very interesting—or should I say revealing?'

His eyes glittered. 'What the devil are you suggesting?'

'Nothing—nothing at all,' she assured him hastily while wondering why her tongue lacked control. Of course he'd know what Megan's room was like. Hadn't he known the family for years? Yet even as she pondered these facts she turned to Megan and said, 'Your room will be next to Leon's. Surely *that* should compensate?'

Leon caught the implication. 'Again I ask, what are you suggesting by these snide remarks?' The question was now accompanied by a scowl.

'Nothing—nothing at all,' Sara repeated, then added hastily, 'But Megan is right. I should have attended to that bedroom before now. It can't remain unused and dominated by Jane's things for ever.'

She left the room hurriedly, and as she went towards her own room she was gripped by the depressing knowledge that Leon appeared to be more than happy to have Megan with them. Suspicion took over, causing her to wonder if he'd known that this girl with the lovely face and flaming hair would be arriving instead of her mother.

Was it possible he had even arranged for this to happen, because after all, where was the man who needed a woman who talked non-stop? Yes, that was it, she decided, her dejection deepening. Leon had wanted Megan to be here, rather than her mother.

When she reached her bedroom her clothes were snatched from the wardrobe and carried into the front room. The drawers of the dressing-table and tallboy followed suit, to be emptied on to the bed, and as she replaced Jane's dressing-table articles with her own, her eyes filled with tears.

'Dear Jane,' she said in an audible whisper, 'if you had to go, you had to go—but the situation you've left is becoming more difficult every moment. What shall I do, for heaven's sake?'

Even as she asked the question the answer flashed into her mind, perhaps because she knew exactly what her great-aunt would have said. Pull yourself together, Jane would have commanded. Get rid of your self-pity. Megan will need clean towels as well as clean sheets and pillowcases. As for Leon—give yourself time to learn what he has in mind. And you'd better wash your face before they see traces of tears.

'Yes, Jane,' Sara answered meekly, her voice holding sadness, then she turned to face Leon who had come to the doorway unheard.

'Yes, Jane?' he queried, looking at her doubtfully.

'I—I was just thinking aloud,' she said, turning away from him.

'You weren't holding a conversation with a spirit?'

'Of course not,' she retorted crossly. 'Although I must admit I feel Jane's presence very strongly when I'm in this room.' Then, changing the subject, abruptly, she asked, 'Where is your *friend*?'

If he noticed her emphasis he ignored it while informing her calmly, 'Megan is in the kitchen, throwing herself into the job. She looked in the fridge and in the deep-freeze, and has now decided on what we shall eat this evening.'

'Well, that's something. At least I don't have to worry about it,' said Sara coldly.

'I'm glad you appreciate that small fact.' He stepped closer to stare down into her face, his eyes searching. 'You've been crying,' he accused softly.

She returned his stare defiantly. 'Can't I shed a tear for someone I've lost? Is that so unusual?'

'No, so long as the tears were not there because of Megan. I've no wish to see you upset by her.'

'You're trying to fool me into believing you could care two hoots about that?'

Irritatingly and without denial he said, 'You'll have to decide for yourself on that point.'

'Then allow me to assure you that Megan is not one of my favourite people. However, she appears to be one who holds a high place in your affections.'

'What makes you so sure about that?' he asked calmly.

'You can call it womanly intuition,' she said loftily.

'I prefer to call it silly imagination,' he retorted.

Feeling irked, she said, 'I can only presume that Megan is capable in the kitchen.'

'Don't you mean in the bedroom?' he teased softly.

'Kitchen was the word I used,' she returned, her tone frosty.

He gave a satisfied smirk. 'She should be—she's a cordon bleu cook.'

'Is that so? Then I'll buy her a blue ribbon to wear at the stove. But no doubt you knew about her ability when you arranged for her to come instead of her mother.' The last words came bitterly.

Leon surveyed her through slightly narrowed lids. His jaw tightened, causing a small muscle to flicker in his cheek. 'Am I to understand you're making a definite accusation?' he queried, his tone frigid.

Sara found difficulty in looking at him, but she managed to say, 'It's so obvious it sticks out a mile.'

'This highly vaunted woman's intuition again, I suppose?'

'You could say so,' she admitted. 'It seldom lets us down.'

'It's a pity it can't point your thinking in the right direction,' he gritted scathingly.

She grasped at the hint of a denial. 'You mean you didn't arrange for Megan to come?'

'Why should I trouble to do that? I can visit Megan whenever I like.'

'But that's not the same as living under the same roof.'

He stared at her in silence before he shut the door, then moved closer to take her in his arms. Holding her against him, he murmured in her ear, 'Is it possible that you're just a teeny weeny bit jealous?'

'*Jealous?* Certainly not!' she gasped indignantly, making a futile attempt to wriggle free from the strength of his embrace, which had its usual effect of making her pulses race.

Leon chuckled, tipping her head back while his lips traced the line of her jaw until they found her throat. A throb in her neck caught his attention, and from there they made their way to claim her mouth, where they nibbled with gentle teasing.

Sara felt the thud of her heart and the explosion of blood through her veins. Her lips parted to the seductive deepening of his kiss, and even if she had had the power to struggle against him, she had no wish to. Instead she gave herself up to wallowing in the joyous sensations that swept through her senses, and, closing her eyes, she basked in the sweetness of the moment.

Nor was she able to resist the pressure and gentle kneading of the firm hands that massaged their way down her spine to clasp her buttocks and drag her sensually closer to his hard muscular body. His arousal called to her, sending sparks through her entire being, and she knew that had they been alone in the house she would have gone under, not only to his need to make love, but also to her own.

But suddenly it ended when she heard the sharp intake of his breath as the strength of his arms left her body. Her eyes flew open as his hands went to her shoulders, their strong grip pushing her away from him, and she saw that his face had become inscrutable. Dazed, she watched as he turned abruptly and left the room.

His departure left her feeling bereft, and, going to the window she gazed unseeingly at the shimmering water and distant hills beyond the lake. Questions buzzed about in her mind, and it was then that she recalled that he had not actually denied arranging for Megan to come instead of her mother. Instead he had sidestepped the issue with a display of affection, making it obvious he had no wish to discuss the situation between Megan and himself.

Almost blindly she turned to face the room's chaos—which was rivalled only by the confusion in her own mind. Vaguely, she knew she must make a start on regaining order, and to do this suitcases for Jane's belongings must be fetched from the cupboard in the laundry.

As she carried them through the kitchen she heard the echo of Megan's laughter coming from the living-room. The sound held a ring of happiness which served only to twist a spear of resentment in Sara's mind, and as she returned to the bedroom she knew she was filled with a biting jealousy that left her feeling shaken.

It gnawed at her, causing her to bang the cases on the floor with sufficient force to bring Leon back to the bedroom, and although she knew he was leaning in the doorway appraising her efforts, she was unable to meet his eyes. Nor was she pleased by the flush she knew to be creeping into her cheeks, but if he noticed it he made no comment.

Instead he asked casually, 'What will happen to all this clothing?'

She was glad of an impersonal topic. 'Most of it will be sold for Jane's favourite charity, the Save the Children Fund. Sorting it will occupy my evenings during the next week.'

'Not completely, I hope. We'd like to share a little of your company.' His tone was nonchalant.

'By *we* I presume you mean you and Megan,' she said, making an effort to speak in an offhand manner that indicated she was barely interested. At the same time she noticed he made no attempt to come near her. Did this mean he was deliberately keeping his distance?

He eyed the suitcases, then demanded with a touch of irritation, 'Why didn't you ask me to carry those cases in for you?'

'Because I'm not entirely helpless. Besides, you were busy entertaining your *friend*.' She stopped, furious with herself for having uttered those last words.

His face was expressionless as he said, 'Megan is about to serve dinner.'

A sudden reluctance to sit at the table with them caused her to say, 'I—I don't really feel like eating. I'm not hungry.'

'That's because you're in a bad mood,' he said in a tone that was almost a reprimand. 'The least you can do is to come and eat what's been prepared.'

'You're very bossy,' she snapped.

'Only when people need to be bossed,' he retorted, then added, 'Wash your hands, and don't be too long about it.'

'I'm not a child!' she flared with a surge of indignation.

'Then stop behaving like one,' he mocked.

Sara sent him a baleful glare as she went to the bathroom, where she contemplated a deliberate delay, but moments later she had shrugged off her peevishness and had gone into the living-room, to be greeted by the delicious odours of an appetising meal.

Megan was obviously satisfied by her efforts, because she smiled happily as she said, 'I found herbs in the garden. I've never had so many at my disposal.'

Sara said, 'Fresh herbs are so much nicer than the dried ones that come out of a packet.'

Megan ignored the remark by directing her answer to Leon. '*We* appear to have all the ones I like to use.'

We——? Sara sent her a glance of enquiry. She had caught the emphasis on the word and wondered if it was meant to include herself with Megan and Leon. She warned herself not to be unduly touchy, and made an effort to control the growing irritation caused by the sight of Megan taking over the role of hostess.

The feeling of being an outsider—or even not in the room at all—became more intense as Megan directed her remarks solely to Leon, who listened with an inscrutable expression on his face.

'I do all sorts of things with herbs,' she told him eagerly.

'Like what?' His tone was full of doubt.

'Oh, I make herb butters of different flavours with chervil, chives, garlic, parsley or sage, and even rose petals.'

He frowned. 'You'd better understand that I prefer plain New Zealand butter, and I'm darned sure I don't fancy rose petals spread on my toast.'

'I don't do that,' she assured him hastily. 'I merely store wrapped butter in an airtight container with strongly scented rose petals for twenty-four hours.'

'The dark red rose petals.' Sara put in, making an effort to join the conversation.

Megan ignored the comment as she continued to speak to Leon. 'You'll love the cheeses I make with marjoram or sage or thyme. And garlic juice is delicious in cottage cheese——'

'But only if one likes garlic,' Sara cut in, making another attempt to take part in this culinary discussion.

Again Megan ignored her as she questioned Leon. 'Do you like caraway seed cake? I'm always careful to not overdo the seeds. And did you know that marigold petals can be used in scrambled eggs?'

'Not in my scrambled eggs, thank you very much,' Leon warned her sharply. 'There's no need to go over-board just because you have so many herbs at hand.'

'How's your meal?' Megan asked sweetly.

'Excellent, of course,' he approved.

'You didn't object to that quick chervil soup,' she cooed. 'And don't tell me you didn't enjoy the veal in mustard and dill sauce, or the sweet basil chopped into the silver beet.'

Leon looked slightly bewildered. 'No, of course not. It was all quite delicious,' he conceded.

Megan's smile reflected triumph as she removed the plates, then she said. 'You'll probably wonder about the small blue flowers floating on the fruit salad. It's borage, and you can eat them. They contain calcium, potassium and a saline, which makes it a useful herb for people who shouldn't be taking salt.'

Sara spoke hesitantly. 'The early herbalists declared that if borage is chopped into silver beet or cabbage it's supposed to bring happiness and comfort, and to drive away melancholia.'

Megan regarded her loftily. 'I know exactly how to use borage—and I must say I'm becoming thoroughly tired of hearing you chip in with your limited knowledge.'

The words were sufficient to infuriate Sara, causing her to spring to her feet and snap at Megan, 'You've got a nerve! I'll have you know it's only through me that you're here, sitting at the table with the man you refer to as your—your——' She choked on the word fiancé, which she seemed unable to utter.

'*Shut up!*' hissed Megan, alarm leaping into her green eyes.

Sara drew a long deep breath as she turned to Leon. 'So much for this trial period—and for the hand of friendship,' she said scathingly. 'Can't you see it's impossible to achieve with your—er—*friend's* constant antagonism towards me?'

'Sit down and take it easy, Sara,' he soothed.

'Take it easy indeed!' she echoed, flinging his words back at him. 'Then hear this—I have no intention of putting up with her attitude, which you don't seem to notice. And I'd like you to remember that but for Jane, *you* wouldn't be here either.'

'But for Jane, nor would you be here,' he reminded her. 'But I can understand that her loss has hit you,' he added gently, reaching across the table to clasp her hand.

She snatched it away, refusing to be placated by either his touch or his tone, and, glaring at him, she snapped scathingly, 'It's a pity you're unable to understand that I'm also hit by what her loss has brought me.'

'I presume you mean this situation?'

'Of course I mean this situation. Nor am I amused by your—your tolerant acceptance of your friend's manner towards me.' Her tears of frustration were being held back only with difficulty.

Leon turned to Megan, his tone still mild. 'What the hell gets into you, Megan? One would imagine you object to Sara's presence in the house.'

Megan gazed at him steadily, a slight flush rising to her cheeks as she said frankly, 'Dearest Leon, can't you realise that I've been quite shocked to find another woman in this house? It's something I didn't expect. I was given to understand that you'd inherited this cottage and that you needed my help. Naturally I came at once.'

'I explained the situation to Edith quite clearly,' he rasped.

Megan rushed on as though he hadn't spoken. 'Can't you see, it was our opportunity to be together alone, but instead, *she's* here. Oh, it really is too bad!' she finished on a wailing note.

Sara, who was still standing, cut in abruptly. 'You can be together now, because I'm going to my room. So make the most of it. Tomorrow I shall go to the employment agency and ask for a suitable person to be found. In the meantime I've had you in a big way, Megan Sellwood.'

'Oh, no, no!' Tears welled into Megan's eyes as she turned to Leon, her manner pleading. 'Please talk to her!'

Perhaps it was the sight of the tears that forced Leon to take control. Speaking sternly to Sara, he said, 'I asked you to sit down. You haven't finished your meal. There's dessert——'

'Sorry, I'm afraid it would choke me,' she admitted, glancing towards the three small crystal sweet dishes standing on the oak sideboard. Each was filled with fruit salad topped with whipped cream and a decoration of small blue star-shaped borage flowers.

'Try and enjoy it,' he urged with a smile. 'You yourself said those flowers are from what's supposed to be the herb of gladness. Give them a chance to drive away your depression, and then you'll remember your promise to give this situation a trial. I know you'll not break your word on that point.'

'How do you know?' Megan demanded doubtfully.

'Because Sara is a person who keeps her word,' he declared with confidence, his brown eyes favouring Sara with a steadfast gaze.

His words were sufficient to make her sit down again, and as she ate her dessert she wondered if Leon really considered her to be reliable, or was he merely soothing her ruffled spirits? It was not that his opinion of her really mattered, of course, although for some silly reason she preferred it to be positive rather than negative.

Nor did she allow herself to dwell on the question of why this should be. Instead she pushed the thought from her mind, and moments later she had left the table to continue the task of sorting clothes. Jane's garments were in excellent order, she decided as she folded a lilac suit made of pure wool, then a shadow caused her to look up to discover Megan watching her from the doorway.

The green eyes swept a look of interest over the clothes, then she said, 'I've come to say I'm sorry.'

Sara's lip curled. 'Sent by Leon, no doubt.'

Megan hesitated, then admitted, 'He felt I should explain the situation more clearly.'

Sara was only vaguely interested, yet felt compelled to ask, 'What situation would that be?'

'It concerns our mothers,' Megan began carefully.

'I don't see what your mothers have to do with your rudeness towards me.'

'You might not be aware of the fact, but they were very close friends from childhood.'

'So what? I'm missing the point.' Sara's tone was abrupt.

Megan betrayed exasperation. 'Can't you understand? Their dearest wish was that Leon and I should marry.'

'And that gives you the right to refer to him as your fiancé?'

'They even told us about it when we were very young,' Megan said, a pathetic note creeping into her voice.

Sara tried to feel sympathy for Megan, but was unable to do so with any degree of honesty. Nevertheless her voice softened as she said, 'The delay puzzles me. Leon appears to have had plenty of time to make a commitment, so what's kept the wedding bells silent? Neither of you are getting any younger. You yourself must be at least——'

'If you must know, I'm twenty-nine and have no wish to be reminded of the fact,' Megan snapped peevishly. 'The trouble has been our lack of opportunity to be together alone. Mummy, with her constant chattering, has always been hovering in the background.' She paused, then sent Sara a significant look before adding, 'I'd make it worth your while.'

Sara's delicate brows rose. 'I don't understand. Worth my while to do what?'

There was a slight hesitation on Megan's part before she said, 'To leave us alone, of course. To get out of the house for a while.' Her tone became pleading as she went on, 'Couldn't you take a few days off while you go home to see your parents? I believe they live in Auckland.'

'Who told you where they live?' The suggestion that she should leave Megan alone in the house with Leon had roused Sara's anger.

'Leon told me, of course, otherwise how would I know?'

'You've discussed this idea with him?' Sara watched her closely.

Megan looked away. 'Well, not thoroughly,' she admitted. 'But I'm sure he'll think it's a good one, especially if you let him think it's your idea.'

'But it's *not* my idea, so why should I lie about it? Personally I doubt if you've discussed it with him at all. I can understand that he sent you to apologise for your rude attitude towards me, but I don't believe he told you to make this explanation about the wishes of your mothers.' Sara paused, glaring at Megan with indignation, then went on in a sharper tone, 'What you're really saying is that you want me out of the house so that you can coax him into your bed. You've got a nerve!'

Megan tossed her head with a show of defiance. 'I can assure you he won't need much coaxing.'

'Been there before, has he?' The thought of Leon in Megan's bed infuriated Sara to such an extent the words were out before she could stop them.

'No, actually, there's been no opportunity for us to sleep together,' Megan admitted on a wistful note.

Sara felt cheered, but she persisted, 'Are you saying that over the years Leon couldn't have made such an opportunity?'

Megan avoided a direct answer by saying, 'There's never been an occasion when we could remain together for a period.'

Sara's spirits rose again as she sought for more comfort in her own mind. If Leon had desired Megan he could have possessed her years ago. Nor would she herself have been held so ardently in his arms if, at heart, he had been longing for this red-haired woman whose beauty was undeniable.

Megan interrupted her thoughts by speaking in a pleading tone. 'Will you do it? Will you take a few days off and go home?'

The last words riled Sara. 'You appear to be forgetting that this is my home. In any case, I'm unable to go to Auckland.'

'Why not, for heaven's sake? Are your girls in the salon so unreliable you can't leave them for a few days?' sneered Megan, her frustration causing her face to become flushed with anger.

'It has nothing to do with the salon. It's Leon and this cottage. At present they make it impossible for me to go away.'

'What on earth are you talking about? I'd take care of your old cottage—and of him,' Megan added with a sly smile.

Sara became impatient. 'You don't understand. Decisions concerning the fate of the cottage must be made. Promises to my great-aunt must be kept, although Leon has other ideas.'

'Promises to *Aunty*!' Megan scoffed in a voice that echoed the utmost scorn. 'I think you're being quite ridiculous—or have you forgotten she's no longer here?'

'That's the last thing I'm likely to forget,' Sara said coldly.

Megan went on, 'As for Leon, surely you realise his knowledge can only be superior to your own. You really must give him credit for knowing the best course to take, unless——' She fell silent, her eyes narrowing as she regarded Sara with sudden suspicion.

'Yes? Unless what?' Sara paused while folding a blue cardigan.

'Unless you have another reason for not wanting to leave this place while Leon is in it.'

'Another reason? Such as what?'

'Such as you yourself becoming emotionally involved with him.'

Sara put the cardigan in the case. 'I don't know what you mean,' she said without looking at Megan.

'I think you do. I believe you've already fallen in love with him.' Megan's voice was hard and accusing.

Sara forced a laugh. 'I think it's a little too soon for that, especially as I hadn't laid eyes on him before last Saturday.'

'Love can strike quite unexpectedly,' asserted Megan, watching her closely.

'Or it can take years—as with Leon in your own case,' Sara reminded her pointedly.

The green eyes flashed. 'Leon *does* love me. It's—it's just that he hasn't realised it yet.'

'You're saying he's too dim-witted to do so?'

'Of course not. It's still at the—brotherly stage,' Megan maintained with confidence.

'Perhaps you're mistaking a brotherly affection for something deeper. It could be easy to do so.'

'Oh, no, it's simply that he's undemonstrative.'

'I haven't found him so——' Sara began unguardedly, then closed her mouth abruptly.

'What do you mean by that?' hissed Megan.

'Nothing—nothing at all,' gasped Sara, annoyed with herself.

'You'll tell me at once!' Megan's clawed fingers snatched at Sara's arm, spinning her round to face eyes that had again become narrowed with suspicion.

'Mind your own business,' snapped Sara, dragging her arm free.

'This is my business, in case you've forgotten——' The words died on Megan's lips as Leon's voice came from the doorway.

'Do I detect an argument?' he drawled. 'What's going on?'

Megan recovered herself instantly. Stooping to whip up the blue cardigan from the suitcase, she lied, 'Yes, we were becoming rather heated over this garment. I thought it might fit me, but Sara says it wouldn't. I wanted to try it on——'

Leon's voice became crisp. 'She's right. It would be too short in the arms for you. Jane was a petite person, whereas you're tall.'

'I know I'm the rather graceful willowy type,' Megan almost simpered, then asked, 'Did you come searching for me?'

He continued to frown as he looked from one to the other. 'I thought a walk along the lakefront might be pleasant.'

Megan's face lit. 'How lovely! I'll come at once.'

Leon looked at Sara. 'I meant the three of us.'

'Three's a crowd,' she reminded him. 'If you'll excuse me, I'd prefer to stay here and continue with getting this room in order.'

'As you wish,' he retorted tersely.

It was not what she wished at all. But how could she tell him she longed to walk along the lakefront with him—but not with Megan causing her to feel *de trop*?

A short time later she stood at the window straining her eyes against the glare of the last of the sun's rays.

She could see them only vaguely, and apart from their distant figures the narrow pumice beach was now deserted; then, as they disappeared from sight, she leaned her forehead against the coolness of the glass pane while dejection descended like a dark cloud from above.

The fact that she could no longer see them seemed fraught with significance. It was like a peep into the future—a vision that filled her with depression as a question raised its head. Would Leon fade from her sight in a similar manner? When the question of Rosemary Cottage had been solved, would he return to Auckland, never to be seen again by herself?

The thought caused an unbearable pain somewhere near her heart, and although she tried to ignore it by getting on with the job, it persisted. And then Megan's words echoed in her mind. *Love can strike quite unexpectedly.* 'But not in this case,' Sara muttered aloud. 'Leon Longley will not sweep me off my feet at a moment's notice.' Unless he has already done so, an inner voice seemed to whisper back at her.

CHAPTER EIGHT

THE rest of the week passed hazily for Sara. She moved from client to client, her nimble fingers working automatically as they put rollers in hair for sets or perms, or styled with the scissors. She knew that Megan was at home in the cottage, proving herself to be a capable housekeeper and cook—but in what manner was Leon proving himself? How was he filling in his time?

Nor did she care to voice the question when she reached home each evening. Instead, she could only curb her curiosity when she found him to be evasive about his day's activities. He'd been looking here and looking there, was the only satisfaction he would give.

But while Leon's inscrutable expression told her nothing, Megan made no secret of her own bubbling satisfaction. Was her happiness real or feigned? Sara wondered dismally as she watched the animation in Megan's face.

And then Friday arrived, and with it came Mrs Coates, a small brisk woman who hurried into the salon with a mouth tight with suppressed anger. The sight of her startled Sara, who had forgotten she would arrive at the cottage as usual, her job being to clean the windows, the floors, the oven or any other chore that needed attention.

Mrs Coates sat in a chair waiting for Sara to finish combing out the head she was styling with a blow-wave, but at last she was able to voice her grievance. 'Don't you want me no more?' she demanded bluntly. 'I went to the cottage as usual, but you seem to have another woman there—a hoity-toity madam who sent me about my business. Told me I wouldn't be needed no more, she did.'

Sara looked at her blankly while searching for words. 'I'm so sorry, Mrs Coates,' she apologised. 'I should have come to see you, but I'm afraid the changes put it out of my head.'

'Changes? Of course I know poor Mrs Patterson has gone——'

'It's more than that, and I'm hoping it's only a temporary situation, but you see, I don't own the cottage entirely,' Sara explained.

The small woman's eyes widened. 'Are you saying Mrs Patterson didn't leave it to you after all?'

'That's right. I'm only a part owner,' Sara admitted.

'But she told me on several occasions that when she went——'

'Yes, I know, but apparently she had second thoughts about it.'

'Well, you could knock me down with a feather!' declared Mrs Coates.

'It came as a shock to me too,' Sara admitted.

Mrs Coates went on, 'I spoke to Mrs Radcliffe next door. She'd seen me arrive, and she guessed I'd leave quite soon, so she was waiting for me at the gate. She said there's a man in the house, but I didn't see no man.'

'Didn't you see a white car in the garage?'

'No. But I can tell you the woman who gave me short shrift was in a real bad mood. Snapped my head off, she did, although I don't think it was the sight of me that put her red hair in a knot. Is that its real colour, or does it come out of a bottle?'

'A rinse helps to keep it looking bright,' Sara told her, then asked, 'Are you sure you didn't see a white car?'

Mrs Coates snorted. 'If my eyesight's good enough to see dust and cobwebs, it's good enough to see a car of any colour. I don't need it to knock me down before I know it's there.' She paused before uttering a sigh of resignation. 'Well, I suppose I'd better get busy and find another job for Fridays.'

Sara said quickly, 'I'll pay you for today and for the next four Fridays, Mrs Coates. By that time I should know more about my own situation, and if things work out in a suitable manner I'll come and see you.'

'Suitable manner?' The woman's eyes were alive with curiosity.

Sara said hastily, 'Would you like a cup of coffee, Mrs Coates? Pam or Dawn would make one for you.'

Mrs Coates murmured her gratitude. 'Thank you, that would be nice. I've pedalled a long distance on me bike.' Her eyes still held questions as she went on, 'That white car you mentioned—would it belong to the man Mrs Radcliffe said is living in the house?'

'Yes.'

'Oh, well, she said he drives away from the cottage every morning quite soon after you've left for work, and he doesn't come home before late in the afternoon. So that's why I didn't see no white car in the garage, or anywhere else, for that matter.'

The information brought a smile to Sara's face. It lifted her spirits and enabled her to see the situation at home more clearly. She had wondered about the activities of Megan and Leon during her absence, and the thought of Leon with his arms about Megan, kissing her as he'd kissed herself, had nagged sufficiently to send her into a state of seething frustration.

No wonder Mrs Coates had found Megan in a bad mood, she thought. Obviously the beautiful redhead had expected to find herself enjoying day after day of Leon's company while he spent a holiday period in his recently inherited Taupo cottage. But this idyllic bliss had not blossomed into reality.

Instead, Megan had found herself left alone and faced by household chores while he went about his business. No doubt he was discussing land for sale with various estate agents, or perhaps he was driving about the district while he considered the potential of various areas for property development. At least he was not at home making love to Megan, and the knowledge caused Sara's spirits to soar even further skyward.

'Thank you for that enlightening snippet of information,' she murmured at Mrs Coates' departing back as the woman, having enjoyed three cups of coffee, left the salon.

The next day found Sara at her usual Saturday task of listing supplies to be ordered. The salon had closed at midday, and as she sat at the reception desk her mind flashed back to this same period a week ago. Was it only a week? It felt more like a year.

The memory caused her to glance at the door, and as she did so the sight of Leon's brown eyes again peering at her through the glass caused a startled gasp to escape her. But this time they had a different effect on her, because they made her heart thump and the blood race through her veins.

Different, too, was her attitude towards him, and instead of being evasive she called, 'Come in, the door's unlocked.'

Leon entered the salon and stood before her, his feet planted firmly apart. His tailored navy shirt and trousers gave him an air of distinction, while his stance spoke of male domination. 'You're coming to lunch with me,' he stated without preamble and as though reminding her of a prearranged engagement.

'Am I?' she queried weakly. 'Isn't Megan expecting us both home for lunch? She knows the salon closes on Saturday afternoon.'

'Megan has learnt to expect me when she sees me,' he informed her with lofty nonchalance.

'You've hypnotised her into this state of acceptance?'

He ignored the question by saying, 'I thought it high time we had a talk. I've scarcely seen you during the week. The moment the evening is over you disappear into your room.'

'I presumed I was doing you a favour,' Sara told him frankly.

'What are you talking about?'

'I understood that you—er—longed to be alone with your friend. Isn't that why you arranged for her to come here?' Then, suddenly alarmed by the thunderous look on his face, she said hastily, 'In any case, I've had things to do.'

'Like what? I can't see that sorting the belongings of one elderly woman would occupy every evening until bedtime.'

'I've also had letters to write,' she prevaricated. 'It's been necessary to acknowledge the flowers and cards that have been sent. Besides, not for one moment did I imagine you'd miss my presence, especially as I could hear Megan's trills of happy laughter echoing through the walls.' It was difficult to keep the irony from her voice.

He came closer to lean over the desk. 'It might surprise you to learn that I've missed your presence. I understood the necessity of your absence during the first two or three evenings, but since then I've considered it to be deliberate. I've suspected it to be a form of escape.'

Sara stared down at the list she had been compiling, yet asked with a touch of defiance, 'From what would I be escaping?'

His voice became accusing. 'From the need to talk about the fate of the cottage. And possibly from Megan—or even from me.'

She could find no reply, because he had hit on the truth in all respects. There had been no need for every evening to have been occupied so completely. She *had* been dodging the issue of the cottage. And she was also avoiding Megan, whose attitude of thinly veiled irritation was making her feel like an outcast. As for Leon himself, her feelings towards him had become so confused she had decided to steer clear of him.

He stood watching her in silence until his patience evaporated. 'Well, have you made up your mind to come with me? I've reserved a table at Cherry Island.'

'Only if you'll let Megan know we won't be home for lunch,' she said, still avoiding his gaze. It was ages since she'd been to Cherry Island, and the prospect of going there with Leon gave her a flutter of inner excitement.

She watched as he pressed buttons on the desk phone beside her, and saw the frown on his face as he listened to Megan's voice echoing through the receiver. It was easy to guess that Megan was furious, but she made no comment until they reached the peaceful island which rose out of the Waikato river only a short distance from the Taupo township.

Tentatively, she said, 'I know Megan was angry. I could hear her voice screaming through the phone.'

'There was no need for her to get so mad,' said Leon. 'I'd already told her not to expect me home for lunch, but the fact that you wouldn't be there either roused——'

'Her suspicions?' Sara cut in. 'No doubt I'll hear about it, if I'm brave enough to go home.'

'Don't allow it to spoil your lunch,' he advised as they reached the car park beside the bridge that spanned the river. Beyond it lay the modern chalet on the island park.

Halfway across they paused to look down at the turbulence of water rushing between rock-lined walls, and as they did so she felt Leon's hand rest on her shoulder. Its pressure caused a sharp intake of breath, and she found herself unable to resist looking up at him.

His eyes smiled into her own as he said, 'I'm afraid we're about three months too late to enjoy the beauty of the cherry trees in blossom. Did you know they cover half the island?'

She caught his relaxed mood. 'Then we'll just have to look at the variety of birds and baby animals, and the rainbow trout that are quite gorgeous when seen through the underwater viewing windows.'

Paintings were on display in the chalet, and as they wandered from one to another Sara found herself to be in a haze of contentment. Leon's company was pleasant, she realised, wishing she could have met him in different circumstances.

A short time later as they sat at the restaurant table those same circumstances were underlined when he said casually, 'I've had a report from the builder.'

Sara's eyes widened as she became wary. 'Builder? What builder?'

'The one from whom I decided to obtain an unbiased opinion of the state of the cottage. Didn't you realise it's something that must be done?'

'No, I—I hadn't given it a thought.'

'Then it's high time you did so.' He paused before going on in a matter-of-fact tone, 'This report can be relied on. I mean, it can be taken as official.'

'I see.' She stared at her plate as doubts began to crowd the back of her mind, then she gave a short laugh. 'This man is one of your close friends, I presume?'

Leon eyed her sternly, his mouth hardening. 'Do I detect a subtle accusation behind that question?'

Sara sought for words but remained silent.

'Are you suggesting I'd instruct him concerning the report?' he pursued relentlessly, his eyes glinting with anger.

Again she said nothing.

'I can see the thought is nagging at you, so why not be honest and admit it?' he rasped.

She nodded, feeling miserable. 'I couldn't help wondering—— '

'By doing so you're insulting my integrity as well as his,' Leon pointed out coldly. 'However, there's nothing to prevent you from acquiring professional opinions of your own accord. Possibly it would be as well for you to do so.'

'Yes, I suppose I could do that,' she conceded, feeling better because the suggestion had come from him, rather than having to declare that she would attend to it herself. 'I'm sorry if I've really annoyed you.'

'It's your distrust that gets under my skin,' he gritted. 'Perhaps I should have told you I was having this inspection made, but I didn't see the need to consult you about a matter that was in your own interest.'

'*Your* own interest, is more like it,' she flung back at him, then, curbing her anger, she demanded, 'So what did this man say?'

'If you'll simmer down I'll tell you. Naturally, he was able to make an accurate guess at the age of the cottage because I'd told him it was built by Samuel's father.'

She nodded, fearing that what she was about to hear concerning the state of the cottage would not be the best of news.

Leon went on, 'The building is still on its original totara timber piles—or rather, what's left of them— which is why the floor is uneven in some parts and creaks loudly in other places.'

She frowned, waiting to hear the worst. 'What else? There must be more, even if money has already been spent on its maintenance.'

'You can bet your life there's more,' he told her grimly. 'Numerous boards should be replaced because of borer or rotting timber in odd places, although the roof seems to be in good order.'

'How nice to know we have a roof that's not about to collapse on our heads!' She tried to keep the sarcasm from her voice.

Leon spoke bluntly. 'The report also states that demolishing the cottage would enable two holiday units to be built on the land. You could live in one and rent the other, or you could find a flat nearer town and rent them both.'

She felt confused. 'Are you saying you've changed your mind?' she asked.

'About what?'

'About living in the cottage while working from an office in Taupo.'

He looked at her quizzically. 'For Pete's sake, did you imagine I intended to move in permanently?'

'That's the impression you gave me,' she retorted.

'I think there's been a misunderstanding. I meant to stay in the cottage only until I'd found an office and had established a man in it. Surely you would realise that?'

'Then—then you don't intend to live in Taupo?' Vaguely, Sara was conscious of a sinking feeling. Where was the relief that should have been flooding her?

'Perhaps I wasn't very clear in explaining that I have my own home in Auckland—inherited from my grandparents.'

'You haven't told me anything about it,' she reminded him.

'You haven't given me much opportunity,' he pointed out drily. 'It's on a hillside and has unrestricted views of yacht races and harbour shipping. I'm unlikely to abandon it for a derelict cottage in Taupo, especially one with continuous hassles attached to it.'

Sparks of anger flashed from her hazel eyes. 'I won't have our cottage referred to as derelict! There are years of life left in it.'

Leon regarded her with interest. 'You're actually beginning to think of it as *our* cottage?'

'I'm making an effort to face up to the fact,' she told him coolly, then, as a thought began to niggle at her, she said with forced sweetness, 'Do tell me about your other house. Do you live alone in it, or is Megan a permanent guest?'

'Nothing of the sort,' he snapped, his jaw tightening. 'I have a married couple living with me. They prepare my meals and give the house any attention it needs. Nor can I understand why you imagined Megan would be in residence.'

She shrugged, then lied, 'Actually, I haven't given any thought to your private circumstances.'

'Which means you haven't been interested in me as a person.' The brown eyes regarded her searchingly as he went on, 'Yet at times I've thought there was a spark of interest in your attitude towards me. Or was that just the need for comfort?'

Sara flushed, knowing he referred to those moments when he had held her closely. 'I must admit recent events have thrown my mind into a state of chaos. Surely you can understand that during the last week I've not known what to think, not only through the unexpected change in my living conditions, but through—through other things as well.'

'What other things?' The question was snapped at her.

'Oh, this, that and the other,' she retorted evasively. How could she tell him about the impact he himself had had upon her? This time last Saturday she had been desperate to get him out of the cottage—but now, just as she was becoming anxious for him to remain in it, he spoke of leaving.

Changing the subject, she asked almost unwillingly, 'Does Megan approve of your married couple?'

The question took him by surprise, his dark brows rising as he demanded, 'Why should she approve of the way they run my home?'

'Well, naturally, I thought——' The words faded away.

'I know exactly what you thought,' he snapped crisply, making no effort to conceal his irritation. 'Nor am I unaware of Megan's aspirations—but let me assure you there's never been even the vestige of a romance between Megan and myself. Nor is it remotely possible.'

His words gave her a sense of relief that was almost overwhelming, and, probing further, she said, 'I must confess I thought you'd arranged for Megan to come to us—I mean instead of her mother.'

'You were mistaken—and I must say these constant insinuations are beginning to bore me. May we have an end to them?'

'Very well,' she agreed meekly.

He went on, 'At least she filled the gap in giving you the required extra woman in the house. Or have you forgotten your fears for your reputation?'

Sara looked at him in silence, finding herself unable to admit she no longer cared about what the neighbours would say. What did their opinions matter when compared with the importance of learning to know this man better?

And now the opportunity of forming a closer relationship with him was about to be lost. They must come to an agreement over the cottage, and as soon as he had made decisions concerning an office in Taupo he would return to Auckland. He would disappear from her life, perhaps never to be seen again.

But not out of Megan's life, she realised. Megan would continue to have access to him in Auckland. She would have opportunities to be near him, and, given time, she might achieve what Leon, moments ago, had declared to be impossible.

His voice came softly. 'Your expression indicates unhappy thoughts—caused by the demise of the cottage, I suppose.'

A sigh escaped her. 'The loss of it makes me feel sad.'

'As you say, there's still life in the old place, so it won't happen immediately.'

'That's something for which I'm thankful. You've had me fearing it would be pulled down the day after tomorrow,' Sara confessed.

He laughed. 'You're forgetting we must wait for probate to be granted, but in the meantime you must realise that—eventually—its end will come.'

She sent him an accusing glare. 'And you'll be glad to see it go, leaving free a valuable lakeside plot of land for one of your own development schemes.'

Leon's expression became pained. 'Please give me credit for having at least a little sentiment for the cottage built by my great-grandfather.'

'You actually do feel for it? Well, I *am* surprised!'

'Of course I feel for it,' he retorted testily. 'Didn't I stay in it as a child? You appear to imagine I'm completely devoid of all sentiment!'

'I'm sorry, I hadn't realised.' Then she sighed again, her voice echoing sadness. 'Nothing stays the same. Everything comes to an end.'

'Except love. They say true love never dies.'

His words surprised her. 'I'm not an authority on love,' she shrugged.

'I suspect you loved Jane, otherwise you wouldn't have stayed with her, especially as you couldn't have had much in common.'

'I became very fond of her—and I was grateful for the refuge she offered in my time of need,' Sara admitted without looking at him.

'Which means you loved—what's this fellow's name—Terry?'

'At the time I *thought* I loved him.' The confession came with reluctance.

'And now?' Leon watched her closely.

'Now it's the thought of Louise, who was my friend and who became his wife, that springs up to face me.'

'That doesn't mean your love for him is completely dead. It merely indicates that you're still running away from the issue, and when your pride gets over its jolt you'll stop running and take another look at him. You'll be back to square one.'

Irritated, she said, 'If you don't *mind*, my relationship with Terry Purvis is the last thing I want to discuss, so can we change the subject? Suppose you tell me how far you've progressed with establishing a Taupo office.'

'It's all under control. I've rented office space, and I've now arranged for it to be managed by one of the Auckland staff. He has a girlfriend in this area, so it will suit him nicely.'

Her spirits sank. 'Does this mean that your—your stay at Rosemary Cottage will now be limited to an even shorter period than you'd intended?' she asked.

He sent her a mirthless smile. 'Aren't you really asking how long it'll be before I get myself out of your hair?'

'You're no longer in my hair,' she found herself admitting in a low voice while unable to meet his eyes.

He made no attempt to hide his surprise as he exclaimed, 'Well, that's a change of attitude!' Then he added on a quiet note, 'But I doubt that the same can be said about Megan, so if you're patient you'll see our departing backs next weekend.'

'*Next weekend?*' Her voice echoed dismay.

'You'd prefer we left sooner?' The question came grimly.

'No, of course not.'

'Yet I detect no ring of gladness. Quite the opposite, in fact. Is it possible you're actually becoming friendly with Megan?'

'Not even remotely possible,' Sara declared with more sharpness than she intended, then she stared at her plate, having suddenly lost her appetite. How could she explain that, while Megan's departure would bring delight, his own would bring only depression?

Nor was it easy to define the reason for what Leon had declared to be her own change of attitude. Nevertheless it was there, and as she recalled their moments of closeness she knew that her feelings had taken a different direction. They had developed depths of their own and were now beyond her control.

Had she known him for only a week? Was a week long enough to learn that she loved him? The knowledge stunned her, and as she continued to stare unseeingly at the table she knew she would always love him, and that there would never be anyone else for her.

Had this been Jane's intention when she had deliberately thrown them together? If so it had been a wasted effort, because it was obvious that Leon had no real depth of thought towards herself, otherwise he would not be so keen to return to Auckland. Nor would Jane have realised that Leon's ambitions would lean towards demolishing her beloved cottage and replacing it with modern buildings. Two holiday units, the man had said.

Leon's voice pierced the gloom building itself within her mind. 'You're full of deep thoughts. Care to share them with me?'

Sara shook her head. 'They're a jumbled mass which circle round Jane and the cottage,' she told him evasively.

'And us?' he prompted gently.

'Yes. You and I are like ships that have collided briefly.'

'Damage has been done?' The brown eyes were watchful.

'A little.' She did not go into details, such as the damage's being mainly to her own heart. Instead she said, 'Like most ships, you'll sail your way and I'll sail mine. Your life will remain unaltered, whereas mine—will never be the same again.' She fell silent as she fought an overwhelming misery brought on by the thought of life without Leon.

However, the tears pricking her lids were mercifully stemmed when he pushed his chair from the table and said, 'If you've finished your coffee we'll take a stroll before we leave.'

'That would be nice.' The suggestion enabled her to stand up, and, blinking rapidly, she moved to examine some of the paintings on the wall. Then, with the tears under control, she turned to him and said, 'We came here to talk, remember? You've had sufficient discussion?'

'I think so. I've stated the facts,' he declared as though that was the only thing necessary. 'I'll give you the builder's report when we reach home. The condition of the cottage will then become quite clear to you.'

'I see.' A sigh of resignation escaped her. It was useless to argue with him, she realised. His forceful character would ensure that what he considered should be done *would* be done. And that would be that. Finish. No more to be said.

It would also mean the end of all she had held dear over the last four years. Despite the presence of Leon and Megan, Sara had felt Jane's spirit hovering about the rooms, and although she told herself that this was sheer imagination, it was something she wanted to hold on to. But soon it would be goodbye, Jane, goodbye, cottage, goodbye, herb garden. It would also be goodbye, Leon, and suddenly she knew that this would be more distressing than the rest put together.

The stroll they took led them along tracks that twisted through native bush where overhead branches sheltered them from the heat of the sun. In one secluded area Leon paused to place a hand on Sara's arm, and, turning her to face him, he said, 'You're unhappy. I can sense your depression coming through loud and clear.'

Her resentment bubbled. 'Then you should also be able to sense that your builder's report has made me hopping mad. Or did you imagine it would make me jump up and down with delight? Or does it amuse you to see my life turned upside down?'

'You're exaggerating. It's only an alteration to your living conditions——'

'Which I've no wish to see changed.' Sara stared up into his face, her eyes darkened by the deep hurt seething within her breast. 'You don't seem to care two hoots about the frustration and inconvenience your precious decisions will cause me.'

'You're mistaken. I care more than you realise.' His hands moved to her shoulders, drawing her closer to him, then slid down her sides to rest on her hips.

His touch made her melt, causing her to feel weak as she heard him whisper her name. His head lowered, and she raised her face to meet his lips. Her arms rose to curl about his neck, and as his fingers pressed into her buttocks she felt the thump of his heart against her own.

The resentment of a few moments ago vanished as she clung to him, while her newly awakened love made her revel in the knowledge that he wanted her. Only with an effort did she refrain from whispering the words against his lips, the words that would tell him she loved him, and instead she gave herself up to an abandoned and joyous response to his embrace.

At last she became aware that he had taken her face between his hands and was staring into her eyes with an intentness that held questions. 'Are you trying to tell me something?' he demanded, his voice husky with emotion.

Embarrassed, she realised she'd been too revealing, and, unable to reply, she hid her flushed face against his shoulder. Then, pulling herself together, she muttered, 'I think it's time we went home.'

'Home? The word has a comforting ring about it, like security. Yes, let's go home.' But he made no move to leave the secluded area that hid them from prying eyes. Instead he kissed her again, his lips brushing gently against her own until his arms tightened about her and the kiss deepened into one of passion. However, it ended abruptly as he took a grip on his control. 'Home,' he repeated with determination.

Sara looked at him uncertainly. 'You do mean the cottage?'

'Of course. Where else?'

'Well, apart from comfort and security, home has a permanency about it, and the life of the cottage now seems to be limited.'

'Ah, you've resigned yourself to that fact?' queried Leon.

'Not entirely.' She looked at him in silence for several moments, her eyes full of questions, then she asked frankly, 'Is that what those kisses were about? To bring me to a state of resignation?'

'You're accusing me of insincerity?'

'To be honest, I don't know what to think,' she admitted in a small voice.

Yet despite these doubts her step was light as they made their way back to the car. Her spirits remained high, and it was almost as though she still clung to the clouds she had recently left.

Leon took his seat behind the wheel, then turned to fasten Sara's seat-belt. As he did so his hand cupped her breast, his thumb gently stroking a suddenly taut nipple. 'Tell that rosebud to hold itself in readiness to be kissed,' he ordered nonchalantly.

'Certainly not!' she gasped, conscious of the deep flush staining her cheeks. His action and words had stirred an unexpected desire, while the thought of his lips on her breast had sent tingles racing wildly through her nerves.

The drive home took only a short time, although Sara wished it could last for hours. During it she sat in a dreamy haze, revelling in the memory of Leon's arms about her body, the feel of his lips on her own. From the corner of her eye she saw his hand leave the wheel, then drew a sharp breath as she felt its pressure on her leg. She knew it made a tentative move towards her thigh, then she smiled inwardly as it was called to order and returned to the wheel.

They were almost home when Leon spoke casually. 'We appear to have a visitor.'

Sara gathered her wits and peered ahead at the vehicle blocking the entrance to the cottage driveway. Its presence caused Leon to leave the Daimler on the roadside, and as they walked past the red sports car she said, 'Perhaps it belongs to your builder friend.'

Leon uttered a short laugh. 'That's unlikely. I doubt if he can rise to owning a Porsche.'

A Porsche. Sara stood still, gripped by apprehension. Terry, she recalled, had made no secret of his desire to own such a car. 'The day will come when I'll drive a Porsche,' he had been in the habit of declaring with confidence. Had the day arrived?

Apparently it had, because they discovered him lounging at ease in the living-room while being entertained by Megan. The glass of Scotch in his hand and the almost empty decanter on the table beside him accounted for his heightened colour. He stood up as they came in, then strode across the room to Sara.

Snatching her to him, he kissed her forcefully on the mouth, then said, 'Darling, where have you been? You *knew* I was coming to see you——'

CHAPTER NINE

FURY gripped Sara as she sprang away from the tall fair-haired man. 'I—I didn't know you were coming,' she stammered while taking in a swift glance of Leon's suddenly narrowed eyes.

Terry sent her a mirthless grin. 'Of course you knew. I rang the salon and left a message. Perhaps the girl forgot to give it to you,' he added with a scowl.

'Neither Pam nor Dawn ever forget to write down a message,' Sara defended. 'There was nothing on the pad.'

Terry shrugged. 'Oh, well, it doesn't matter. Megan has been very sweet to me. She even provided me with lunch.'

Megan flashed a smile at him. 'It was a pleasure. When the expected ones don't come home for lunch it's nice to know the food one has prepared won't be thrown out.' The words were accompanied by a reproachful glance directed at Leon.

'And the wine she served was exactly right, old chap,' Terry put in with satisfaction. 'I trust you weren't keeping it for a special occasion.'

Sara felt slightly hysterical as she surveyed the tightness about Leon's mouth, plus the frosty glint in his eyes which told her it had taken only seconds for Terry to get under his skin. Was this because Terry had been entertained by Megan? Or was it because of the manner in which she herself had been embraced? Sadly, she doubted if the latter was the cause.

Terry went on smoothly, his eyes resting on Sara, 'As you can guess, I've come to see the great inheritance. Megan has been quite voluble about it. Apparently it doesn't belong to you entirely, and when you've sold your share to her fiancé they'll use it as a weekend holiday house.'

Megan flushed as she drew a sharp breath and said quickly, 'I didn't exactly say Leon is my fiancé.'

Terry made no attempt to hide his surprise. 'Didn't you? But you definitely implied it. In fact, I thought you made it very clear indeed.'

'I made nothing clear,' protested Megan, her face turning an even deeper pink. 'When you were probing to learn how Leon, Sara and I fitted into the situation of the cottage I told you Leon and I had always been very close.' She moved to stand beside Leon, and looking up into his face she almost pleaded, 'Isn't that so, Leon? We've always been—*very close*.'

'We've known each other since childhood,' he admitted gravely.

Terry said, 'Sara and I have also known each other for years. Once we were very close, and then there was a hitch, but we have every intention of becoming close again.'

Sara gasped at the temerity of the statement. 'That's what you think,' she snapped at Terry.

Unperturbed, Terry spoke to Leon. 'I trust you'll give her the true value of her share. The cottage is obviously old, but we all know that lakeside land is worth a lot of money.'

'The property is about to be valued,' Leon told him abruptly.

'No doubt by one of your own cronies?' Terry's words held a hint of veiled suspicion before he added, 'You'll understand I must make sure of fair play—on Sara's behalf, of course.'

Leon's voice became icy. 'Aren't you forgetting it's an estate? Procuring the valuation is in the hands of the solicitor—or is it beyond you to understand that small fact?'

Terry's face cleared. 'Of course—I *had* forgotten. Sorry, old chap, if you thought I was beginning to suspect, but Megan had been so definite about your purchase from Sara, and that it would be a hideaway from the worries of the business world. A little old love nest, I've been given to understand.'

'*I did not say that!*' Megan almost shrieked.

'You didn't have to,' Terry said complacently. 'The situation spoke for itself, especially when you said your fiancé had arranged for you to come here. Now you can't deny giving me that interesting piece of information.'

'You've been drinking too much of Leon's whisky!' Megan hissed at him, and with a swift movement she swept the decanter from the table beside him, replacing it in the cabinet.

Sara had become conscious of growing horror as she listened to the words burbling from Terry's lips. She noticed that his face had a rosier hue than usual, and that the decanter's whisky line was at a low ebb. Obviously he had had sufficient to loosen his tongue, and was now at the uninhibited stage of not caring what he said.

A feeling of nausea gripped her as the pieces fell into place, and she began to wonder if Leon had lied to her about his association with Megan. Despite his assurance that there had never been a vestige of romance between them, she now suspected they were much closer than he had admitted. And even if a commitment had not yet been made public, it was probably standing in the wings waiting to be announced—after the question of the cottage had been settled.

But why be so secretive about it, unless he thought his relationship with Megan would affect his dealings with herself? In a desperate effort to clear the situation in her mind Sara moved to the window, where she stood with her back to the others, gazing sightlessly across the lake.

And then Leon's voice spoke beside her. 'Are you in a daydream?' he demanded.

The mistiness in her eyes made it impossible to turn and face him. 'Daydream?' she repeated in a dull voice, continuing to stare beyond the lake at the distant rise of mountains.

'Your friend Terry said he's taking you out to dinner this evening. Twice I've asked if this is true, but you've made no reply. Nor have you said anything about these arrangements,' Leon accused without making any attempt to hide his annoyance.

'Haven't I?' She continued to stare out towards the lake. 'Well, some people are very secretive about their— their association with others. They're experts at hiding the truth.'

He frowned. 'What's that supposed to mean?

'You should know.' She turned to glare at him reproachfully, unaware of the inner hurt reflected in her eyes which still held a suspicion of glassiness. 'Not even remotely possible, you said.'

'I don't understand. What are you talking about?'

'I'm referring to your romance with someone it's unnecessary to name,' she said in a voice too low for the others to hear.

'Ah, the thought of it irks you?' he grinned, a note of quiet satisfaction creeping into his voice.

'Not at all,' she lied. 'It's just that I dislike being assured about something that isn't correct.'

But within her heart her love for Leon urged her to deny her suspicions and make excuses for him. Yet the reasons for his reticent attitude came through with certainty. Obviously, if she agreed to sell her share to him he could do as he wished with the property. No doubt he would follow the builder's suggestion of replacing the cottage with two holiday units, one being for himself and Megan.

And in the meantime Sara herself was being handled with care until she agreed to sell. She was being played along like a trout on a line until she complied with his wishes. Then, as though to contradict her own thoughts, she recalled his words at Cherry Island. It's your distrust that really gets under my skin, he had gritted.

Yet, despite those words, what value could she place on Leon's kisses? None at all. What depth of feeling lay in the closeness or pressure of his embrace? Again—none at all. There was only emptiness, she warned herself as, overwhelmed by misery, she swallowed while endeavouring to fight back tears that stung her lids with sharp prickling sensations. A fine fool she'd look if they began to roll down her cheeks.

Leon spoke in her ear. Almost as if reading her thoughts, he queried in a dry tone, 'Why not try to trust me?'

How she longed to do just that, she thought, sighing within herself, then keeping her voice even she said, 'I shall, when I know I *can*. Until then I'll have to rely upon information from—other parties.'

'Such as from Megan—and from your friend?'

'Terry knows only what she's told him,' Sara pointed out. 'And we both know that where there's smoke there's fire.'

'Which means that the smouldering ashes Terry had for you have been rekindled,' said Leon in a low voice. 'Every intention of becoming close again, was what he said.'

'If he thinks he can take up from where he left off, he can think again,' Sara muttered in an undertone.

'Why not give him the chance to prove himself?' Leon suggested.

'Certainly not,' she snapped, hurt by the fact that he would even put such an idea into words.

'Or at least give yourself a chance to prove that your own feelings for him are completely dead. That's if they really are dead,' he added significantly. 'Perhaps they're just lying dormant under a thick layer of ashes that only needs brushing away.'

'You're suggesting I should give Terry the opportunity to brush them away?' Sara asked in a small tight voice.

'At least you'd be sure——'

'I am sure. Believe me, they died four years ago.'

Terry's voice spoke from behind them, his tone jocular as he said, 'There's a lot of mumbling going on beside this window. Are you deep in conference, or have you discovered a view you haven't noticed before these last few minutes? Megan and I are beginning to feel left out in the cold.' His mouth hardened as his pale grey eyes slid from Sara to Leon.

Megan spoke sweetly. 'She's probably making up her mind about what she'll wear on this very special occasion.'

'And you haven't told her what time you'll call for her—in that racy Porsche,' Leon reminded him smoothly.

Terry looked eager as he put an arm about Sara's shoulders. 'Then you've agreed to come out with me? You seem to have taken so long making up your mind I was beginning to wonder if you'd even heard me say I'm taking you out to dinner.'

She moved from within the circle of his arm. Typical of him, she thought crossly. No such thing as by your leave or please will you come? Just the same arrogant attitude that expected others to bow to his demands. Terry, she realised, hadn't changed at all, and the knowledge goaded her to say loftily, 'Actually, I haven't yet decided whether it will be convenient.'

Leon said, 'How could it be inconvenient? Apparently you haven't been out with this man for years. He'll have to work hard to make up for lost opportunities.'

Terry scowled. 'Listen, fellow, I know exactly how to make Sara happy.'

Leon's brows rose. 'You do? You could have fooled me.'

'He'll give her a marvellous evening,' Megan put in brightly.

Sara felt like a dummy as she stood listening to the exchange between them. It was easy to believe that Megan wanted to see her spend the evening out with Terry, because that would enable her to be alone with Leon. But why was *he* pushing her along in this manner?

Did he also want to be alone in the house with Megan? She herself had given them plenty of opportunity for intimate talk, hadn't she? During the week she'd spent every evening in the bedroom sorting Jane's belongings, so what more did they expect of her?

A deep and painful breath shook her as she wondered if her presence in the house had restricted them from actually going to bed. Had they feared that creaking floorboards would betray their activities? And then pride came to the rescue, causing her to smile at Terry as she said, 'I'll be ready at whatever time you arrive to collect me.'

'Good,' he said with a grin of satisfaction. 'It'll be just like old times.'

Later, in her bedroom, Sara could raise no enthusiasm from the prospect of going out with Terry Purvis. She cared little about what she wore, and she had to force herself to pay attention to her make-up. After lunching with Leon, the thought of dining with Terry seemed like moving from the sublime to the ridiculous. It was anticlimax.

Nor was she in a hurry to join the others in the living-room, where Leon would be sure to detect her despondency, so she decided to remain in her room for as long as possible. However, she was interrupted by the sound of a knock on the door.

Tightening the girdle of her dressing-gown, she opened it, to be faced by Megan, who stood before her in a filmy creation that wafted about her slender form in a variety of greens. Its neckline was cut daringly low to reveal the cleavage between full breasts scantily encased in a strapless bodice.

The redhead broke the silence as Sara stared at her wordlessly. 'You're not the only one being taken out to dinner this evening,' she said with a hint of smugness.

Sara forced a smile. 'So it seems. I must say you look gorgeous. You're like a woodland nymph.'

'Thank you. Leon says I'll turn a few heads. He's taking me to the Wairakei Hotel,' Megan added with satisfaction. 'I believe that's where Terry has reserved a table, so we'll see each other from across the room.'

'I suppose so.' Sara's depression deepened. She had no wish to be presented with the view of Leon entertaining Megan. The evening would be difficult enough without that spectacle thrown in.

Megan said, 'I see no reason for us to join forces during the evening. I'd prefer you to stay with Terry while I remain with Leon.' The words were snapped in the form of an order.

'I doubt if you'll have any worries on that score,' said Sara in a dull voice, her eyes resting on Megan's cleavage. 'Although there's always the possibility that Terry might decide to take a closer look at all you have on display,' she added frankly.

Megan giggled. 'Mummy calls it my flaunting dress.'

'How right she is,' murmured Sara, then looked at the electric hair-roller Megan produced from among the folds of her skirt. 'Was there something you wanted?'

'Yes—I've brought my curling brush for you to give attention to my hair. Leon said he felt sure you wouldn't mind in the least.'

Sara said nothing as she took the roller from Megan and plugged it into the power point near the dressing-table. It took little time to heat, then she invited Megan to sit on the stool before the mirror.

There was a brief silence before Megan said, 'I hope you have something special to wear this evening.'

Sara rolled a small section of hair, then admitted, 'I haven't given it much thought.'

'Then you'd better do so at once. This should be a great opportunity for you.'

Sara's brows rose. 'Opportunity—to do what?'

'To get back with Terry, of course,' Megan exclaimed.

'Why should I want to do that?'

'Because he seems to have done very well for himself.'

'Only at the expense of somebody else,' Sara pointed out, recalling Terry's admission about having done nicely out of the marriage break-up.

Megan's slim shoulders lifted in a small shrug. 'I wouldn't know about that. But I do think you need somebody—and you can forget any ideas you might have had about Leon.'

Sara bristled, her tone cold. 'Who said I have ideas about Leon?'

'Every girl Leon meets has ideas about him,' said Megan. 'I can't see that you're any different from the rest. But of course you understand that I have a prior claim.'

Sara turned to meet the green eyes in the mirror. 'Are you saying you're a little nearer, or that you've clinched the deal?'

Megan smiled. 'With luck, I intend to do it tonight.'

'At the Wairakei Hotel?'

'Where else? A really romantic setting.'

'I'd have thought the privacy of the cottage would have been more conducive to romance—especially with the place to yourselves,' remarked Sara.

Megan sighed. 'Yes, to be honest, I thought so too— but Leon said that as Terry was taking you out to dinner, he should take me. You see, that's what he's like. He didn't want me to feel neglected, so I intend to make it work to our best advantage.'

Despite herself, Sara was interested. 'How will you do that?'

Megan sent a sly smile into the mirror. 'We might spend the night there—in one of the bedrooms.'

Sara's knuckles whitened as she gripped the brush. 'What's wrong with your own bed here in the cottage? Night after night you've had the opportunity.'

Megan drew a hissing breath. 'I'll tell you what's wrong with it. It's in a crummy old cottage where the passage and bedroom floors creak to high heaven—and of course *your* presence in the next room has made it quite impossible for Leon to come to my room.'

'Sorry about that, I'm sure,' Sara snapped crossly as she retracted the teeth of the brush and slid the roller from the last curl. She remained silent as she brushed and arranged Megan's hair into a style which framed and made her face look even more beautiful.

Megan surveyed herself with satisfaction. 'Thank you. You certainly know what you're doing when it comes to hair.' Then she smiled as she added, 'I'm afraid it won't look so perfect after an entire night with Leon.'

Again Sara bristled inwardly, but kept her temper as she said, 'If you'll excuse me, I'd like to finish dressing.'

'OK. Sorry to have held you up, but you'll understand how very important this is to me.' Megan went to the door, then paused to look back. 'If we're not home for breakfast please don't worry about us. We'll be quite happily occupied—at Wairakei.'

Sara's depression deepened as she took her rainbow silk skirt, top and jacket from the wardrobe. She had worn it when going to dinner with Leon, and to wear it when going to the same place with Terry seemed like another anticlimax. But she might as well make an effort to look her best, because Leon would see her from across the room—at least, he would if he could drag his eyes away from the shoulders and cleavage laid bare before him. A flaunting dress! Huh!

Later, as she sat beside Terry while the red Porsche purred its way along the lakefront, she had a feeling of unreality. She knew he sent several side glances in her direction, but she kept her eyes on the road ahead while trying to control her despondency.

Eventually he spoke. 'It feels pretty good, eh?'

'Yes, it runs beautifully,' Sara agreed. 'You must be delighted to own a Porsche at last. I remember you always longed for one.'

'I wasn't referring to the car,' said Terry. 'I'm talking about us. I meant it feels pretty good to be going out together again after all this time. Don't tell me you're not absolutely delighted about it, because I won't believe you.'

His conceit made her smile, but as she had no wish to hurt him by making a crushing retort she merely said, 'It's always nice to be taken out to dinner. Thank you, Terry.'

'Later we shall have a serious talk,' he informed her.

'Oh? About what?' She could think of no serious subject to be discussed with Terry.

'About the cottage, of course. You're far too pliant, far too ready to do as other people want you to do. And now you're about to fall in with this fellow Longley's plans.'

Sara felt indignant. 'Am I, indeed? Who says so?'

'Megan, of course. She became quite chatty after she'd had a few drinks at lunchtime today.'

'I doubt if she told you the entire situation,' Sara said. 'For instance, did she tell you about the promise I made to my great-aunt who previously owned the cottage?'

'Yes. I'm afraid both Longley and Megan look on that as a huge joke. But we'll talk about it later.'

A huge joke. The words infuriated Sara into a silence which lasted until they reached the hotel.

Terry parked the car, then led her into the lounge, where he ordered drinks, and as Sara sat taking small sips from her glass she waited to hear what he had in mind. At the same time her eyes continually scanned the crowded lounge for the sight of Leon and Megan, but she could see no sign of them.

She knew they had been ready to leave when she and Terry had left, yet they seemed to be taking a long time

to make an appearance. Was this because they had decided to go elsewhere? Or was it because they had decided to spend the evening at home in the seclusion of
the cottage, and away from the obligation of making a
party of four?

Terry, she noticed, did not stint himself when or-
dering his own drinks, and by the time they went to the
dining-room Sara could see he was ready to launch upon
the serious talk he had in mind. However, the subject
was not brought up until the wine waiter had poured
champagne.

'This is a celebration,' Terry grinned.

Sara looked at the bottle she knew to be costly. 'Are
you having a spur-of-the-moment birthday?' she asked.

He laughed. 'Of course not. It's just that we're
together again, and that I'm here to guide you.'

'You mean—to take care of my interests?' she asked
with a show of innocence.

'That's right. You always did need someone to point
you in the right direction.'

'I've matured since those days, Terry. I think I can
handle my own affairs—but thank you for your concern.'
Terry's concern, she felt positive, hovered round the
situation of the cottage, and how it could be veered towards his own benefit.

He leaned forward in a confidential manner. 'I'm not
sure you can handle this lot. Megan seemed to be very
definite about what had been planned.'

'Planned?' echoed Sara. Despite her lack of belief in
some of Megan's statements, she felt startled as she
waited to hear more.

He went on, 'Apparently the idea is to pull down the
cottage and build holiday units. Megan showed me the
sketch of a floor plan she had in mind for Leon and
herself. It will be an upstairs apartment, built to catch
the sun and the view.'

Sara tried to ignore the inner coldness that gripped
her, and, pulling herself together, she said, 'Megan's

wishful thinking is inclined to run away with her. I've heard her make statements that are not strictly true.' Or were those statements about Leon being her fiancé true after all? she wondered miserably. *Should* she believe Megan—or *could* she believe Leon? Her love for him urged her to do so, but this was becoming increasingly difficult.

Terry said, 'She was very definite about it, especially when she had the floor plan spread on the table. Of course, no move can be made until probate has been granted by the court, and then you'll find Longley anxious to buy your share. And that's where I come in.'

'You? What do you mean?' she asked.

'Now that we're together again you must allow me to advise you—and to negotiate for you,' he added with satisfaction.

She regarded him steadily. 'Who says we're together again?'

'Of course we are. It's only natural for us to take up——'

'From where we left off?' she cut in. 'You're making a mistake, Terry. I've no intention of turning the clock back. We were together years ago, if you care to re-member—and then you married Louise, in case you've forgotten.' The smile she sent him did nothing to soften the cool accusation in her voice.

His light grey eyes held an appeal for mercy as he said contritely, 'Sara darling, it's not often I eat humble pie, but at this moment I'm chewing a huge hunk of it. Can't you find it in your heart to forgive me? I made a terrible mistake——'

'Which apparently paid off handsomely.'

'Please, I've no wish to go into all that. I just want to help *you*,' he pleaded.

'In what way can you do that?'

'As I said: by advising and negotiating for you.'

'And your advice is?' Despite herself Sara was curious.

'When the time comes, just dig your toes in and refuse to sell. Refuse until he's frustrated to hell, and then leave the rest to me. A soft and pliable woman such as yourself needs a tough fellow like me to handle Longley. He needn't imagine he'll get your share for peanuts. If he wants it he'll have to pay plenty.'

'You're making it sound very unpleasant. I don't believe Leon would try to beat me down,' she argued crossly.

'So now you're defending him,' he sneered. 'Does that mean you have faith in him? Exactly how long have you known this fellow?'

'I believe him to be a man of integrity,' she said evasively, not wishing to answer his last question.

Terry's eyes were penetrating. 'Megan said you've known him only since the old lady's death. I'd say it's a little too soon for him to have pierced your emotional armour.'

Sara found herself unable to look at him as she exclaimed, 'You and Megan certainly found time to discuss my affairs!'

'It was necessary to learn all I could while the opportunity was there. However, if he's wriggled his way into your affections you'll have to face up to the truth.'

Sara asked in alarm, 'The truth? What would that be?'

'You know exactly what I'm saying. If Longley has been stringing you along with words of love you can believe it's for one purpose only. Any kisses he's planted on those sweet lips don't mean anything at all. Do you understand? Not a damned thing.' The last words were uttered with a snarl.

She stared at the food on her plate, feeling unable to eat it. Leon's kisses were still vivid in her mind, but they had been unaccompanied by even the slightest suggestion of love. Stringing her along was the term Terry had used. Had Leon been doing that?

'I dare say he *has* kissed you,' Terry pursued, watching her through narrowed lids. 'He *has* held you in his arms, huh? Perhaps you've even gone further——'

'Mind your own business!' she snapped furiously, then realising he was doing his utmost to goad her into admissions, she stated firmly, 'This subject is now closed. I don't wish to discuss it.'

'But, my darling, you need my help——'

'Nonsense!' she cut in. 'And please remember that I'm not your darling. Also the problem of the cottage is my affair, and I shall handle it as I see fit.'

His mouth took on the obstinate line she remembered so well. 'I can't allow you to do that, Sara. You're sure to make a mess of it. You must be saved from your own foolishness, and now that you've come into my life again I intend to take care of you. We'll begin by announcing our engagement.'

An uncontrolled shriek of laughter escaped her. 'You had the opportunity to do that years ago.'

'Please, let me make up for lost time,' he implored earnestly, and, reaching forward, he lifted her hands from where they rested on the table. A swift movement carried them to his lips, where they were kissed in a tender manner.

Embarrassed, she was about to snatch her hands away when a hasty glance at the other diners showed Leon and Megan at a nearby table. She felt her cheeks burn as she saw him lean forward to mutter a word to Megan, then stand up and come towards their table.

His eyes glowered with a strange darkness that was in keeping with the grim lines etched about the tightness of his mouth. When he spoke there was a harshness in his voice. 'So Megan wasn't mistaken when she assured me that you two have found each other again.'

Terry, who had risen to his feet at Leon's approach, agreed with a happy grin. 'That's right, old chap—she's promised to make me a happy man.'

Sara gasped at the audacity of the statement. 'Don't be daft,' she snapped at Terry, then turned a flushed face to Leon. 'You know very well that Megan's mind is apt to jump ahead of itself——'

Terry broke in, 'My dearest, there's no need for you to deny what Megan has said. You *know* you've agreed to allow me to take care of you.'

'That's a lie—I've agreed to nothing!' gasped Sara as a feeling of desperation gripped her.

'Lies appear to be coming from one of you,' Leon drawled coldly.

'Please don't listen to *him*,' she pleaded, realising that the sight of Terry kissing her hands had influenced Leon's opinion of their relationship, and was no doubt making him believe all that Megan had said.

Terry ignored Sara's protest as he spoke to Leon. 'Surely you can understand that I intend to take care of her—and that any business affairs that come up will be dealt with through me.'

Leon gritted, 'I presume you mean business affairs such as the question of the cottage?'

Terry grinned. 'That's exactly right,' he replied softly.

Sara had heard enough from the two men, who were glaring at each other. Luckily their voices had been kept low, although she feared that diners at the next table were listening with avid interest. Keeping her own voice low, she whispered furiously, 'I intend to handle the matter of the cottage in my own way—and for your interest, Leon, Terry and I are not together again.'

Her last words faded as she realised that Leon had not heard them. He had walked away even as they left her lips, and no doubt he still believed that a reconciliation had taken place between Terry and herself. Frustrated, she turned to Terry and demanded angrily, 'Why did you tell those lies?'

He smirked at her. 'What lies? I don't consider them to be lies. Everything I've said will come true—you just wait and see.' His voice rang with confidence as he refilled their glasses with the last of the champagne. Raising his own, he said, 'Here's to us—together again.'

Sara shook her head. Terry, she realised, had to be given the message, so she said firmly, 'No, Terry, I shall not drink to such a toast, because it will never happen. You made sure of that on the evening you became engaged to Louise.'

'Don't be silly, Sara. That's all in the past, when you were little more than a child. Can't you understand you weren't ready for marriage at that time?'

'At least you're right about that,' she agreed. 'I was too young to judge people. I was living in a dream—in love with a man who was ready to hurt me the moment the boss's daughter gave him a second glance.'

'I've changed, Sara,' he declared earnestly. 'You'll find I'm an entirely different person.'

She forced a smile. 'I doubt it, because people don't change. As the years pass they learn to hide the less pleasant side of their characters, but you're not even making a good job of doing that. Strictly speaking, you're more interested in my inheritance than you are in me.'

His mouth twisted into a sneer. 'While you're more interested in Longley than you are in me. Why not admit it?'

'Would that surprise you?' she asked.

A short derisive laugh escaped him. 'I thought so, but I'm afraid you don't stand a chance with *him*—at least, not with such a gorgeous piece at his disposal, ready and willing to be tossed into bed at the drop of a hat.'

'How can you be so sure about that?' asked Sara in a low voice while Megan's own words returned to her mind.

'Good grief, you've only to look at her! Invitation written all over her. He's probably reserved a room for the night.'

'Will you shut up!' she gasped. 'I refuse to listen to such talk.' Nor was she unaware of the depth of pain stirred by his words.

He went on relentlessly, 'I'm not saying that you yourself are unattractive, Sara. You have a cute little nose and a lovely smile, but against her—well, you should be able to see for yourself.'

Sighing, Sara nodded miserably. 'Oh, yes, I can see it very plainly. I'm unable to hold a candle to her.'

His tone softened. 'There's no need to look so depressed. I'm here, ready and anxious to do anything I can for you.'

'Thank you, Terry, but there's no need——' Her words faded as she looked at the nearby table, where Megan's chatter was bringing a smile to Leon's lips. Even as she watched he turned and held her own gaze, the smile disappearing as his expression changed to a hardness that caused cold fingers to clutch at her heart. It made her feel she'd had enough emotional hassle for one evening, and turning to Terry she said in a pleading voice. 'I'd be grateful if you'd take me home.'

Terry needed no persuading. He stood up abruptly and said with unconcealed eagerness, 'Yes, let's go home. We'll have coffee in the cottage.'

Sara saw the sudden gleam leap into his eyes, but paid little attention. However, when she thought of it later she realised it should have warned her that he had more than coffee in mind. But in the meantime she had one desire only, and that was to leave the dining-room and to run as far as possible from the sight of Leon's attentive attitude towards Megan, or the disapproval he sent towards herself.

CHAPTER TEN

LITTLE was said during the drive home, mainly because Sara scarcely heard Terry's attempts at amicable conversation. Instead, her mind was plagued by the memory of the cold accusation in Leon's eyes.

Nor was it difficult to fathom its reason, she realised. She had assured him that there would never again be anything between Terry and herself, yet this evening he had watched them, to all appearances dining happily in each other's company. According to Terry they were together again, and no doubt this statement would have been cemented in Leon's mind by a few pointed remarks from Megan.

Her depression deepened as she realised the situation put her into the category of being a person whose word could not be relied on—a person without integrity. How could Leon think otherwise? Then, as Terry parked the Porsche in the drive, her thoughts were diverted by the slight movement of the Radcliffes' kitchen curtain. Neighbourhood Watch was at work, she realised.

In her own kitchen she busied herself filling the electric kettle and putting coffee mugs on the trolley, and although she was vaguely aware of a restlessness in Terry's manner she paid little attention to it until she heard the creak of the passage floor and guessed he was prowling through the cottage to make sure they really were alone.

A small twinge of uneasiness touched her, but she brushed it aside, then, as he returned to the kitchen, she said, 'I'm afraid it's only instant coffee. It's all we bother to have.'

He leaned close to her. 'Who needs coffee?' he smirked.

Sara sent him a look of surprise. 'I thought it was what you wanted. Isn't it what we came home for?'

He laughed. 'You've got to be joking! I could think of a more interesting occupation than drinking coffee. Let's go to your bedroom. We could lie on the bed and talk in comfort.'

'Certainly not!' she flashed at him in a furious tone. 'You should know I've no intention of going near a bedroom, let alone lying on a bed!'

'Don't be silly, darling. Why do you think I brought you home if not to seal the fact that we're together?'

'*Stop it*, Terry!' she almost shrieked. 'I'm becoming tired of this nonsense. We are *not* together again, and the sooner you get that fact into your head, the better it will be.'

He moved to put his arms about her. 'Now you listen to me. If I say we're back to square one, that means we're back to square one. A new beginning, you understand?'

She pushed him away. 'No, Terry. I don't understand why you're so persistent about something that can never be.'

'You're just playing hard to get.'

'Please, will you drink your coffee and go home like the good friend I'd like you to be? I'm very tired and I'm longing to go to bed——' Sara realised the last words were a mistake the moment they had left her lips.

He grinned. 'You want to go to bed, huh? Now you're talking sense. You can forget the coffee. I know which is your room, because Megan showed me through the cottage today.' The last words were accompanied by a swift movement that swept her up into his arms.

A gasp escaped her as she found herself being carried like a child towards her bedroom. Her kicks and struggles had no effect against his strength, and he laid her on the bed and stretched himself beside her.

'How—how dare you?' she shrieked, her panic rising as her arms were pinned to her sides and she felt his weight being pressed upon her.

'Simmer down,' he muttered in her ear. 'I've no intention of hurting you. I'll be gentle——'

A long-drawn breath helped to control her temper and her fears. It enabled her to think clearly and to ask, 'You intend to rape me?'

'Rape is an ugly word,' he said, breathing heavily against her neck. 'I intend us to make love like adults who know what they want. Just give me a few minutes and you'll want me as much as I want you.'

'Like hell I will!'

'Be patient, my love. I'll carry you to the heights.'

She lay still, suffering the kisses he pressed on her face and mouth, and even tolerating his hands cupping her breasts.

'That's better,' he murmured. 'You're calmer now. I knew you'd be sensible. Put your arms round me—hold me tightly.'

Her brain whispered that she'd be wise to respond—a little.

Nor was he slow to notice, even if her lack of ardour escaped him. 'Now you're becoming warmer,' he said with satisfaction. 'I knew you would. Just let me get rid of this jacket.'

He sat up and removed it, then flung it on the floor. His shirt and tie followed, and it was as he bent to remove his shoes that Sara jumped from the bed and raced from the room.

Oaths escaped Terry, as half-clothed, he rushed after her, but she reached the kitchen before him, then fled through the garage. He caught her on the drive, where he grabbed her arm and swung her round, but as he tried to lift her, her screams rose on the air.

'Shut up, you stupid little bitch!' he snarled, putting a hand over her mouth while trying to drag her back towards the garage.

She bit his hand and continued to yell, the sound causing lights to flash in the Radcliffe house. Running footsteps pounded on the concrete path, followed by Iris, her husband and rugby-playing son.

Terry dropped Sara abruptly, almost flinging her to the ground before running into the cottage, hotly pursued by the two Radcliffe men. Moments later they returned with Terry sheepishly carrying his jacket and shirt.

'You've left your tie,' Sara pointed out coldly.

'You can keep it as a memento of this fascinating evening,' he gritted at her. 'It'll help you to recall how you led me on.'

'You damned liar!' she shouted. 'Get out of my sight, and don't ever *dare* to come near me again!'

An instant later the Porsche was being backed out of the drive, while Sara turned to the Radcliffes with words of tearful gratitude. 'I've never been so grateful for Neighbourhood Watch,' she admitted.

'He won't be back,' consoled Iris. 'He'll know that Megan and Leon will be home soon. I saw them go out together.'

Sara nodded, feeling miserable. She doubted if Leon would be home soon because, according to Megan, they would be spending the night at the Wairakei Hotel, sharing the same bedroom.

The thought riled her into an irate state of mind which caused her voice to shake as she said goodnight to the Radcliffes and again thanked them for coming to her assistance. Nor did her anger abate when she returned to her bedroom and was met by the sight of Terry's tie lying on the floor. A swift kick sent it flying across the room, where it hit the window before landing near the dressing-table.

Suddenly exhausted, she crawled into bed, but found that sleep evaded her, not because of the ordeal with Terry, but because her mind kept reverting to the thought of Leon and Megan at Wairakei. Would they spend the night there?

The answer came next morning when she found them having breakfast in the kitchen, her face betraying her surprise as the question slipped out. 'Don't they provide room service at the hotel?'

Leon looked at her wonderingly. 'Room service? Did you expect us to have breakfast there?'

'Well, yes, I was given to understand——'

'That we'd spend the night there? What gave you such an idea?' Leon's voice held curiosity tinged with amusement.

Megan cut in quickly, 'It probably came from Terry. Isn't that so?' She sent a look of appeal towards Sara.

Sara met her eyes steadily. 'No, it did not come from Terry.'

Leon's voice hardened, his tone demanding an answer. 'In that case, where did it come from? You must have got it from somewhere.'

Sara spoke coldly. 'That's something you'll have to work out for yourself. It shouldn't be too difficult.'

He regarded her in silence, then spoke in a voice that was still cool. 'I trust you had a happy evening with your friend.'

Sara sent him a bleak glance. 'If you don't mind, I have no wish to discuss last evening.'

Leon's lips thinned. 'Why not? I thought you were having a fantastic time, having your hands kissed in full view of the public.'

The silence that followed his words was broken by a giggle from Megan, who watched Sara with a malevolent gleam in her eyes.

Leon went on, his tone sardonic, 'Perhaps you can explain something I find difficult to understand. It's about—cold coffee.'

'Cold coffee?' Sara echoed incredulously, turning puzzled eyes from Leon to Megan while waiting to learn more of whatever was simmering in their minds.

His voice was grim. 'When we came home after midnight, there it was on the bench, two mugs filled and ready to be enjoyed, except that by then it was stone cold. Why would that be?' His dark brows rose as he waited for an answer to come from Sara.

But before she could find words Megan cut in rapidly. 'I told you why last night,' she reminded him, running long fingers through her red hair. 'It was because something more important cropped up—like going to bed. After all, who wants coffee when they have the cottage to themselves?' she added with a shrill laugh.

Sara felt apprehension taking a firm grip. There was more to these questions than met the eye. 'Is that what you think?' she demanded, turning to Leon.

His answer came coldly. 'Purvis said you were together again.'

'You believed him?' She felt cold all over.

'He seemed to be quite definite about it, if you remember.'

Her chin rose. 'I recall denying his words. Why do you choose to believe him rather than me? Is this male chauvinism?'

Megan spoke with satisfaction. 'He believes Terry because the coffee mugs spoke up loud and clear.'

Sara turned on her angrily. 'What sort of nonsense is this? I suspect that the only person to speak up loud and clear would be yourself. When you saw the mugs on the bench your imagination began to work, causing you to jump to wrong conclusions which you planted in Leon's mind. And he believes you,' she added bitterly, turning accusing eyes upon Leon.

Megan sent her a smile of forced sweetness. 'Oh, I think we have a little more than imagination and vague conclusions to rely on for the truth of the matter.'

Sara spoke to Leon, her tone weary. 'Please ask your *very* dear friend to be more explicit.' Then, as he continued to look at her in silence, she noticed that his frown had deepened while the lines about his mouth had become grim. Distrust was written over every inch of his face, causing her apprehension to become even more acute.

Megan's voice continued to drip honey as she played her trump card. 'Lovers who want to hide their activities should never be careless enough to leave evidence lying in full view,' she sneered with satisfaction.

Sara felt bewildered. 'What do you mean?' she asked.

The smug tones continued. 'While you were in the shower I passed your bedroom. You'd left your door open, and something lying on the floor caught my eye. I went in and picked it up—and guess what it was?' she ended on a note of triumph.

Sara felt sick as enlightenment dawned.

Megan's next actions came swiftly. A drawer was snatched open, an article extracted and thrown on the table. 'Terry's tie, I believe,' she exclaimed with an air of even greater triumph.

Sara stared at the length of dark material which seemed to condemn her. 'Yes, that's Terry's tie,' she admitted in a dull voice, the mere sight of it bringing back the previous evening's trauma.

Leon rasped, 'Divested himself of it in your bedroom, did he?'

Megan gave a ringing laugh. 'And not only his tie! I'll bet his shirt and trousers were ripped off right smartly. Little Miss Purity sure had you fooled, Leon.'

Sara began to shake with rage. 'How *dare* you make such suggestions?' she snapped at Megan.

Megan went on, her voice rising as she spoke to Leon, 'When they left so early I told you they were going home to bed. You didn't believe me—but now you *know*!'

He regarded her curiously. 'What made you so sure of it?'

'I'd let it be known that you and I would be spending the night at the hotel. She simply fell into my trap. She imagined she and Terry would be alone in the cottage all night. If we hadn't met your tiresome Auckland friends we'd have been home earlier. We'd have discovered them in bed together——'

Sara felt nauseated. If they'd come home early enough to witness the bedroom scene, what would Leon have thought?

His voice gritted at Megan. 'You planned to do this? Really, I had no idea you could be so devious!'

Her tone became pathetic. 'Leon, darling, can't you see that I did it for *us*? I fear she's constantly on your mind, occupying the place that I should have——' She stopped, realising she had said too much.

Leon spoke gently. 'You'll always be a close friend, Megan.'

She took a deep breath, then blurted out frankly, 'I want to be more than that. Have you forgotten your mother's dearest wish?'

'Of course not. But I don't intend that it should rule my life. I shall marry the woman of my own choice.'

Megan hissed maliciously, 'I doubt if your mother would approve of one who'd taken a man to bed under your own roof——'

'It is not his roof!' Sara was stung to cut in.

Leon turned on her with a snarl. 'Is this true? You did take him to bed—*under our roof*?'

'What do you think?' The question dripped with icy water.

'Was he in your bedroom?' he demanded aggressively.

She faced him with defiance. 'Yes, if you must know, he was in my bedroom. The tie was given to me as a souvenir. As for the rest, you can believe what you like.'

He eyed her doubtfully. 'Something tells me there's more to this situation than meets the casual glance.'

'There is, but you'd be too blind to see it clearly,' Sara lashed at him, her pride forbidding her to give further explanation.

'Can't we be reasonable enough to talk about it?' he demanded.

Her lip curled. 'I doubt it. Megan has already steered your mind along the course she wants it to take. I shall say nothing to change it. It'll have to do that on its own accord.'

'You're being thoroughly stubborn,' he complained. 'You can at least tell me why you left the hotel so early.'

Sara looked at him through eyes shadowed by pain. How could she explain that the sight of him with Megan had become intolerable? Instead she said, 'I'm afraid explanations would bore you. I'm sure you prefer to examine the plans Megan has been drawing—unless you've already seen them.'

Leon's eyes narrowed. 'Plans? What are you talking about? I know nothing of plans.'

Sara noticed the startled expression on Megan's face, but she went on relentlessly, 'I mean the plans she showed Terry. The plans for holiday units to be built when this cottage has been demolished. I understand that you and she will occupy the better of the two. I trust you'll be very happy in it,' she added bitterly.

'I'll be interested to see these plans,' he said with a touch of grimness underlying his tone.

'I'm sure you will,' she returned sweetly. 'Now if you'll excuse me, I'll do some gardening.'

'But you've had so little breakfast,' purred Megan, her voice full of insincere concern.

'Thank you, I've had sufficient. I'm feeling in need of a spell out in the sun where the air is fresh and free of spite and intrigue.'

Leon spoke quickly. 'No, Sara, don't go out yet. I feel we should get this matter sorted out.'

'To what purpose?' she demanded abruptly. 'It's obvious your sympathies are with Megan, and even if you say you know nothing about her unit plans, I doubt if I believe you.'

He glared at her angrily. 'Why do you say that?'

'Because you yourself mentioned holiday units, so there's little need to wonder if you know about the plans.

You've probably helped her to draw them—*Mr Property Developer*!' she finished scathingly as she left the room.

In the garage she found her small fork and kneeling pad, and as she carried them towards the herb garden she wondered how long she would be able to tolerate the present situation. Her main problem lay in being able to decide what she should do, while against this lay the question of what she *could* do.

For her own peace of mind the number one priority lay in getting rid of Megan, and to do this she had only to exert her right as part owner of the cottage. But how would Leon feel about that? If he loved Megan sufficiently to want her to be there, what could she herself do about it? Above all else she wanted Leon to be happy. It didn't matter about herself. She'd get over it, somewhere in the dim future. Or would she? Only time would tell.

As she cleaned round the lavender bush her thoughts turned to her great-aunt. Jane had tried to control the fate of the cottage from the grave, she realised. But when people died many of their wishes died with them, and Jane had made the mistake of bringing in someone who would not comply with her wishes. So what should she herself do?

The answer came almost at once. Tomorrow she would visit John Abernethy. She would tell him she had decided to sell her share of the property to Leon, and he could prepare the papers for the transfer when probate had been granted. Leon could do as he wished with the place, but she had no wish to watch it being done, so she would go back to Auckland.

The more she thought about it, the more convinced she became that it was the right course to take. 'Sorry, Jane,' she mumbled while dragging at weeds, 'I'm afraid you've placed me in an impossible position. If I hadn't fallen in love with Leon it would have been different. But you're no longer here, and his happiness is important to me. Please understand, Jane, wherever you are——'

Leon's voice spoke in her ear. He had arrived unnoticed and now squatted beside her. 'You're holding a conversation with yourself?'

Sara glanced at him through tear-blurred eyes. 'Yes. A sign of madness, you think? Not the full pint, as they say?' And definitely daft to have fallen in love with you, she chided herself in silence.

He regarded her closely. 'You've been crying. Your eyes tell me.'

'What of it? When I talk to Jane I'm allowed a few tears.'

'You also shed tears last night. Iris Radcliffe phoned to ask how you were after last night's ordeal. I hesitated to admit that I didn't know what she was talking about, but she went on to enlighten me. Suppose you tell me more—such as the whole story.'

'I doubt that either you or Megan would be even remotely interested,' she told him bitterly. Then her lip trembled as she added, 'Unless it would amuse you both—especially your dear friend to whom you would recount the incident. She'd find it quite hilarious.'

'You're so sure I'd do that?' he gritted.

'It would give you both something else to laugh about—a continuation of last night's gaiety.'

'You appear to have very little faith in me,' he declared coldly.

'How can I have faith in a man who kisses me and holds me close only for a set purpose of his own?' The words came with a rush.

'That set purpose being the acquisition of the cottage, I suppose.'

She sighed, then said sadly, 'You're actually admitting it?'

'I'm admitting nothing,' he rasped. 'And I must say your imagination does you credit.'

The reply that rose to Sara's lips was silenced by Megan's voice rising on the air as she approached. 'Leon darling, you haven't finished studying my plans.'

A mirthless laugh escaped Sara. 'Imagination, did you say, Leon *darling*?'

Megan spoke to Sara, her tone full of forced brightness. 'Will Terry be here for lunch? I presume you have much to discuss—like wedding plans, for instance.'

Sara ignored the remark as she turned away to jab fiercely at the weeds. From the corner of her eye she saw Megan take Leon's arm in an effort to hasten his return indoors, and she also saw Leon remove her clinging fingers—but not for one moment was she fooled by his action.

For the next fifteen minutes her agitation grew as she visualised them bending over Megan's plan, their heads together, their shoulders touching. But when she went indoors a short time later she did not discover this to be the case. Instead she found Leon relaxing in the living-room while studying a sheaf of papers.

He stood up as she entered. 'I'm glad you've come in. I was about to fetch you.'

Sara stared apprehensively at the papers in his hand, the sight of them causing a nervous tension to creep through her body.

He waved them at her. 'I think it's time you examined the builder's report.'

Her heart sank. She had no wish to examine the builder's report. It could only spell more depth of depression, especially as it was something that would be used as a weapon against her own wishes to maintain the cottage. 'I don't think I want to see it,' she said.

'But you must see it. It concerns the amount of work necessary.'

She gave a sigh of resignation. He was right, of course. Sooner or later she would have to see it, so she settled herself in a nearby chair while he handed her the papers. And then her eyes blurred as they skimmed passages referring to repiling, replacing guttering and downpipes, and the renewing of timber. The necessary work was much more extensive than she had realised, and at last she returned the papers without a word.

'Well? What do you think?' Leon demanded.

'I—I don't know what to think,' she admitted. 'I had no idea the cottage was in such poor condition. It makes me feel so—so very inadequate.' Then her control broke as a sob rose to her throat. She left the room quickly, almost running to her bedroom, where she flung herself on the bed and wept.

Next morning found Sara in John Abernethy's office.

The elderly solicitor's eyes were full of concern as he looked at her across the top of his desk. 'Are you sure you're taking the right course in relinquishing your share of the property?' he asked.

She nodded miserably. 'It's the only course.'

'Mrs Patterson wouldn't be pleased. I doubt if it's what she had in mind.'

'Really? Then what *did* she have in mind?' Sara demanded sharply.

John Abernethy stared at his desk, and instead of answering her question he said, 'At least you can be sure she'd be most upset if she knew you were abandoning your half of Rosemary Cottage.'

'I can't help it. I can't live there with Megan. The entire situation has got beyond me.'

'Who is Megan—and what is this situation?' he asked, sitting back and preparing to listen.

Sara told him about Megan and the reason for her presence in the cottage, then, unaware of the sadness in her voice, she said, 'I think Leon intends to marry her.'

He looked at her closely, his next words coming bluntly. 'What about you? Are you in love with him?'

Sara was unprepared for the question. She looked at him in startled silence, then, to her horror, her eyes filled with uncontrolled tears. She snatched a handkerchief from her handbag and dabbed at them furiously as she said, 'If Leon's happiness lies with Megan, there's nothing more to be said.'

John Abernethy regarded her with a long and penetrating stare, then he gave a deep sigh as he said, 'This has all the hallmarks of a sacrifice. Very well, I'll attend to the transfer. I'll get the papers ready for when this is possible. You may examine them on Wednesday.'

'Thank you, Mr Abernethy.' Sara looked at him through eyes that were still damp as she added, 'Please believe me when I say I really do feel I'm being a traitor to my great-aunt.'

His tone became abrupt. 'Personally I consider you're being a traitor to yourself. Nor do I approve of your action. You must be very deeply in love with Longley to go to such lengths.'

Her lip trembled, but she made no reply as she left the solicitor's office, and when she returned to the salon she hurried into the back room to splash her eyes with cold water. She felt more than thankful to discover the appointment book promising a busy day that would force her to control her thoughts.

The day ended at last, and with the closing of the salon door her depression loomed to wrap itself about her like a dark cloud. Despite the warmth of the late afternoon she felt cold as she drove home—but here a surprise awaited her. When she walked into the living-room she found Leon pouring a sherry while Megan sat in a chair—weeping.

Sara's amazement pushed her own despondency aside as curiosity took over. 'What's the matter?' she asked after a brief moment of hesitation.

Megan sniffed into a handkerchief. 'I have to go home. Daddy phoned and demanded my return to the office. He's short-handed.'

Leon handed her a glass that was almost brimming over. 'I understood Daddy said he'd allow you a fortnight. Time's up.'

Megan looked at him reproachfully. 'You could have told him you wanted me here. It would have made a difference.'

'Is it necessary?' he asked nonchalantly.

Her tear-filled eyes widened. 'For us to be together? Of course it's necessary.'

Sara sent Leon a sharp glance. Didn't he consider it necessary for them to be together? But he was so enigmatic, so non-committal where romance was concerned, that it was difficult to read his true feelings. She turned to Megan, trying to sound uninterested. 'So—when will you leave?'

'Tomorrow morning.' Her voice held a tremor as she turned to Leon. 'I hate it when we're so far apart. I don't want to be in Auckland while you're in Taupo, more than a hundred and eighty miles away.'

'I'll be in Auckland by the end of the week,' he assured her. 'I've business to attend to, and then I'll be leaving Taupo.'

Sara emptied her glass, then asked sweetly, 'Business—such as arranging for the cottage to be demolished as soon as possible?'

Megan said scathingly, 'She's really quite dotty about this old place, but she'll get over it when she sees the new units.'

Sara remained silent, hurt by the thought of the cottage being torn down, and unable to bear the idea of the new units.

Megan went on, 'By the way, Terry called this afternoon. He came to collect his tie.'

Sara's laugh bordered on hysteria. 'His tie? My precious souvenir—gone?' Her hand shook as she took her refilled glass from Leon.

He spoke to her quietly. 'I was here when he came. He said to tell you he was sorry for the lovers' tiff on Saturday night. He'll be in Auckland for the rest of this week, but he'll return at the weekend to discuss dates.'

Sara was nonplussed. *'Dates?'*

'A wedding date, of course,' Megan put in. 'Leon and I hope you'll both be very happy, don't we, dear?' Her eyes were full of appeal as they turned to Leon with the endearment.

'Of course.' His face was inscrutable.

Sara felt frustrated as she glared at him. 'Why am I unable to convince you of the truth? Only an idiot would imagine I'd marry Terry Purvis.'

'You're saying I'm an idiot?' Leon gritted through tight lips.

'Not a *complete* idiot,' she amended sweetly. 'Given an extra dash of brain you'd be almost half-witted.' Then, feeling emotionally drained, she went to her bedroom, where she spent most of the evening.

Next morning she left for work at an earlier hour than usual because she had no wish to witness the fond farewell she felt sure would take place between Megan and Leon. The day proved to be busy, the brightest part of it resting in the knowledge that Megan would not be in the cottage when she returned home from work.

Later, as she drove along the waterfront road, her thoughts turned to Leon. Had he missed and yearned for Megan during the day? Would he be bored with her own company during the evening? Would he even be there when she arrived home?

Her spirits rose when she saw the Daimler parked in the garage, and when she went into the living-room she discovered him lounging in a chair studying the builder's report. However, he made no attempt to discuss it with her, and her dejection returned as she sensed an aloofness in his manner.

Nor did he thaw sufficiently to enable her to pierce his remote attitude, and by the time she went to bed after an unsociable evening of watching television, she felt they had really drifted apart. But that, she supposed, was to be expected if he intended to marry Megan.

The next day was Wednesday, and with it came her appointment with the solicitor. It had been made for four o'clock, but on arrival she found herself being ushered into a waiting-room. Mr Abernethy was engaged with a client, his secretary explained, but would she please study these papers until he was free?

Sara took the papers and sat down to study the long-winded legal phrasing, but within moments she was utterly confused, because a mistake appeared to have been made. Mr Aberncthy had got it all wrong. This document was not one in which she agreed to sell her share of the property to Leon, it was one that gifted—her eyes blurred as she read it again—yes, *actually gifted* his share of the property to herself.

Feeling stunned, she sat staring at the papers, wondering what she should do, then the door opened to admit Leon, who carried a similar document in his hand. Staring at it, she guessed the only difference lay in the terms of the transfer.

Leon closed the door behind him and said testily, 'That fool of a secretary has made a mess of things. She's muddled the documents.'

Sara felt her legs tremble as she rose to her feet. 'Why have you done this? I can't accept such a gift.'

'It will please me if you'll do so.'

'But—why?' she faltered.

'Because I love you. I want you to have the place.' The admission came bluntly.

Sara felt dazed. Was she hearing correctly? '*You love me?* But I thought—I was so sure——' Her words died away.

'Yes? You were so sure of what?' The question came quietly as he crossed the room and looked down into her eyes.

'That—that you intended to marry Megan.'

'Did I tell you that?' he asked.

'No—but the indications coming from her were clear enough, especially with the plans she'd drawn for units to be built on our property—the best to be occupied by yourselves during weekends.'

'Why did you believe her?'

'Because I'd been given no reason to do otherwise. I thought, if this is where your happiness lies I'd better sell my share to you and let you get on with the job.'

'You were really concerned about my happiness?' he demanded, still staring down into her face.

'Of course. But I couldn't bear to actually watch it happen, so I've considered going back to Auckland.'

'Where you'll marry Purvis?' he rasped.

Sara drew a deep breath. 'Can't you understand I'll never marry Terry? Never, never, *never*!' she declared with force.

'But I understood from Megan that it's all arranged—and Purvis himself was adamant that you were together again.'

'Just as Megan was adamant about your own association with her,' she flashed at him. 'She's referred to you as her fiancé on more than one occasion. Why should anyone think she's lying?'

'Why indeed? Let me assure you I've never spoken to her of marriage, nor have I ever wanted to marry anyone—until I met you.'

She looked at him wordlessly, her heart thumping, her eyes shining. Was she hearing his words correctly? In an effort to remain calm she said, 'I suspect that Terry and Megan are rather alike. They brainwash themselves into believing their own wishful thinking.'

'You're probably right, but if you don't mind I'd prefer to forget them. We have other matters to discuss.' Leon indicated the papers in his hand, then asked, 'If you're willing to consider my happiness, is it possible you love me—just a little?'

Sara nodded, then spoke in a whisper, 'Yes, oh, yes, I love you much more than just a little, Leon.'

He dropped the papers and gripped her shoulders. 'Then please say you'll marry me.' The request came urgently.

'Yes—as soon as possible,' she promised, raising her face to meet the passion of his kiss, his lips fusing with her own. The papers in her hand fluttered to the floor, and as her arms crept about his neck she felt her body being strained against him.

At last Leon murmured, 'Darling, I love you so very much. I hated to see your unhappiness over the fate of the cottage—that's why I was ceding my share to you.' He kissed her again while she clung to him in ecstasy.

But suddenly the spell was broken as the door opened and John Abernethy's voice came to their ears. 'Do I detect a change of plans?'

Sara peeped at the older man from beyond Leon's shoulder. 'Things are slightly different,' she admitted shyly, her face rosy.

The solicitor's eyes twinkled. 'Do I hear the sound of wedding bells in the distance?'

'Distance be damned,' Leon retorted with a grin. 'Near future is more like it. You can shake the moths out of your best suit and be ready to attend the ceremony.'

'I'll be glad to do that,' John told him gravely. 'I'll be there on behalf of Mrs Patterson. It's what she had in mind, of course—or were you both so busy being mad with each other that you failed to realise that salient fact?'

Sara said, 'You can't be saying my great-aunt planned this. She couldn't have known she had so little time left.'

The solicitor looked at her kindly. 'A few bad turns had warned her the sands were running out.'

Sara felt shocked. 'Bad turns? She didn't tell me about them.'

John smiled. 'Ah, but then she didn't tell you everything, did she?' He turned to Leon. 'So what are your plans for the cottage? Demolition or rejuvenation?'

Leon answered without hesitation. 'Rejuvenation, of course. A builder has given me a report on the work necessary to bring it up to standard. His men will begin the job as soon as possible.'

'Isn't your main home in Auckland? A rather grand house with harbour views, Mrs Patterson told me.'

'Yes—but Sara hasn't seen it yet.' Leon put his arm round her as he added, 'But the cottage will always be our special hideaway where we'll spend as much time as possible. Besides, we have a herb garden to care for. Rosemary for remembrance,' he added softly.

Sara was still in a daze when she reached home. She parked her car in the garage, and then Leon, who had followed in the Daimler, closed the doors. In the kitchen she felt as though she walked on air, and as she opened the fridge he put his arms about her.

'We should go out to dinner to celebrate,' he said against her lips, his mouth teasing with gentle tenderness.

She shook her head while her arms encircled his waist. 'Perhaps tomorrow night. This evening I ask only to be alone with you. That's celebration enough for me.'

He held her closely, murmuring endearments until he said, 'Don't you know the danger of being alone with me? Can't you recognise a hungry male who longs to make love with his future bride?'

Sara hid her face against his shoulder while controlling her own desire to lie naked against him.

'There's only one thing keeping you safe,' he said as though reading her thoughts. 'It's my strong suspicion that you'd rather come to me as you are. You'd prefer a first-time wedding night.'

Despite herself she trembled. 'How did you guess?'

'I know you better than you realise, my darling. And let me admit I've been wanting you since the first time I watched you through the glass of the salon door. However, it'll be as you wish.'

'Thank you.' Her eyes shone, then closed as his kisses made her feel slightly delirious with joy. Nor was there need for him to speak of his deep longing, because it spoke for itself.

After several long minutes they drew apart, then Leon said huskily, 'This must stop. I'll pour us a drink.'

Sara followed him into the living-room, and as her mind came down from the clouds her thoughts reverted to the scene in the solicitor's office. 'Don't you think it was strange?' she asked. 'I mean, the way we were given the wrong documents. Lawyers don't usually make such mistakes.'

Leon handed her a sherry, his eyes thoughtful. 'I don't believe that was a mistake. I suspect it was a deliberate ploy to show us the light. And it did. It brought us together.' He raised his glass. 'A toast to John Abernethy.'

'And to Great-Aunt Jane,' Sara added softly.

'And to our own future together.' He took her in his arms again and their drinks were forgotten.

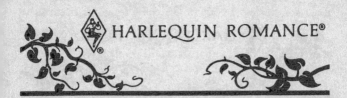

HARLEQUIN ROMANCE®

**Harlequin Romance
invites you to a
celebrity wedding—or is it?**

Find out in Bethany Campbell's
ONLY MAKE-BELIEVE (#3230),
the November title in

THE BRIDAL COLLECTION

THE BRIDE was pretending.
THE GROOM was, too.
BUT THE WEDDING was real—the second time!

Available this month (October)
in The Bridal Collection
TO LOVE AND PROTECT
by Kate Denton
Harlequin Romance #3223

Wherever Harlequin Books are sold.

WED-7

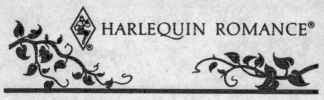

HARLEQUIN ROMANCE®

Valerie Bloomfield comes home to Orchard Valley, Oregon, for the saddest of reasons. Her father has suffered a serious heart attack, and now his three daughters are gathering at his side, praying he'll survive.

Orchard Valley

This visit home will change Valerie's life—especially when she meets Colby Winston, her father's handsome and strong-willed doctor!

"The Orchard Valley trilogy features three delightful, spirited sisters and a trio of equally fascinating men. The stories are rich with the romance, warmth of heart and humor readers expect, and invariably receive, from Debbie Macomber."

—Linda Lael Miller

Don't miss the Orchard Valley trilogy by Debbie Macomber:

VALERIE   Harlequin Romance #3232 (November 1992)
STEPHANIE   Harlequin Romance #3239 (December 1992)
NORAH   Harlequin Romance #3244 (January 1993)

Look for the special cover flash on each book!

Available wherever Harlequin books are sold   ORC-G

Take 4 bestselling love stories FREE

Plus get a FREE surprise gift!

Special Limited-time Offer

Mail to Harlequin Reader Service®

In the U.S.	In Canada
3010 Walden Avenue	P.O. Box 609
P.O. Box 1867	Fort Erie, Ontario
Buffalo, N.Y. 14269-1867	L2A 5X3

YES! Please send me 4 free Harlequin Romance® novels and my free surprise gift. Then send me 6 brand-new novels every month, which I will receive months before they appear in bookstores. Bill me at the low price of $2.49* each—a savings of 40¢ apiece off the cover prices. There are no shipping, handling or other hidden costs. I understand that accepting the books and gift places me under no obligation ever to buy any books. I can always return a shipment and cancel at any time. Even if I never buy another book from Harlequin, the 4 free books and the surprise gift are mine to keep forever.

*Offer slightly different in Canada—$2.49 per book plus 69¢ per shipment for delivery. Canadian residents add applicable federal and provincial sales tax. Sales tax applicable in N.Y.

116 BPA ADLY   316 BPA ADME

Name _____ (PLEASE PRINT)

Address _____ Apt. No. _____

City _____ State/Prov. _____ Zip/Postal Code. _____

This offer is limited to one order per household and not valid to present Harlequin Romance® subscribers. Terms and prices are subject to change.

ROM-92   © 1990 Harlequin Enterprises Limited

HARLEQUIN  PRESENTS®

BARBARY WHARF

Home to the *Sentinel*
Home to passion, heartache and love

The BARBARY WHARF six-book saga continues with
Book Two, BATTLE FOR POSSESSION. Daniel Bruneille
is the head of the *Sentinel*'s Foreign Affairs desk and Roz
Amery is a foreign correspondent. He's bossy and
dictatorial. She's fiercely ambitious and independent.
When they clash it's a battle—a battle for possession!

And don't forget media tycoon Nick Caspian and his
adversary Gina Tyrrell. Will Gina survive the treachery of
Nick's betrayal and the passion of his kiss . . . ?

**BATTLE FOR POSSESSION (Harlequin Presents #1509)
available in November.**

October: BESIEGED (#1498)

If you missed any of the BARBARY WHARF titles, order them by sending your name, address, zip or postal code, along with a check or money order for $2.89 for each book ordered
(please do not send cash), plus 75¢ for postage and handling ($1.00 in Canada), for each
book ordered, payable to Harlequin Reader Service, to:

In the U.S.	In Canada
3010 Walden Avenue	P.O. Box 609
P.O. Box 1325	Fort Erie, Ontario
Buffalo, NY 14269-1325	L2A 5X3

Please specify book title(s) with your order.
Canadian residents please add applicable federal and provincial taxes.

BARB-N

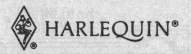

THE TAGGARTS OF TEXAS!

Harlequin's Ruth Jean Dale brings you
THE TAGGARTS OF TEXAS!

Those Taggart men—strong, sexy and hard to resist...

You've met Jesse James Taggart in FIREWORKS!
Harlequin Romance #3205 (July 1992)

Now meet Trey Smith—he's THE RED-BLOODED YANKEE!
Harlequin Temptation #413 (October 1992)

Then there's Daniel Boone Taggart in SHOWDOWN!
Harlequin Romance #3242 (January 1993)

And finally the Taggarts who started it all—in LEGEND!
Harlequin Historical #168 (April 1993)

Read all the Taggart romances!
Meet all the Taggart men!

Available wherever Harlequin books are sold.

If you missed *Fireworks!* (July 1992) and would like to order it, please send your name, address, zip or postal code, along with a check or money order for $2.89 (please do not send cash), plus 75¢ postage and handling ($1.00 in Canada) for each book ordered, payable to Harlequin Reader Service to:

In the U.S.

3010 Walden Avenue
P.O. Box 1325
Buffalo, NY 14269-1325

In Canada

P.O. Box 609
Fort Erie, Ontario
L2A 5X3

Please specify book title with your order.
Canadian residents add applicable federal and provincial taxes.

HARLEQUIN HISTORICAL

CHRISTMAS

• STORIES • 1992 •

Capture the magic and romance of Christmas in the 1800s
with HARLEQUIN HISTORICAL CHRISTMAS STORIES
1992—a collection of three stories by celebrated
historical authors. The perfect Christmas gift!

Don't miss these heartwarming stories, available in
November wherever Harlequin books are sold:

MISS MONTRACHET REQUESTS by Maura Seger
CHRISTMAS BOUNTY by Erin Yorke
A PROMISE KEPT by Bronwyn Williams

Plus, this Christmas you can also receive a FREE
keepsake Christmas ornament. Watch for details in all
November and December Harlequin books.

DISCOVER THE ROMANCE AND MAGIC OF THE
HOLIDAY SEASON WITH HARLEQUIN HISTORICAL
CHRISTMAS STORIES!

HX92R